SPACE 9:

Also compiled by Richard Davis

Space 5
Space 6
Space 7
Space 8
I've Seen a Ghost: True Stories from Show Business
Animal Ghosts

SPACE 9:

A collection of science fiction stories
chosen by Richard Davis

HUTCHINSON
London Melbourne Sydney Auckland Johannesburg

To the memory of Judith Diana King:
with love

Hutchinson Children's Books Ltd

An imprint of the Hutchinson Publishing Group

17–21 Conway Street, London W1P 6JD

Hutchinson Publishing Group (Australia) Pty Ltd
16–22 Church Street, Hawthorn, Melbourne, Victoria 3122, Australia

Hutchinson Group (NZ) Ltd
32–24 View Road, PO Box 40–086, Glenfield, Auckland 10

Hutchinson Group (SA) Pty Ltd
PO Box 337, Bergvlei 2012, South Africa

First published 1985

Set in Baskerville by Book Ens, Saffron Walden, Essex

Printed and bound in Great Britain by Anchor Brendon Ltd, Tiptree, Essex

British Library Cataloguing in Publication Data
Space 9.
   1. Science fiction, English
   I. Davis, Richard
   823'.0876'08 FS   PR1309.S3

ISBN 0 09 158850 2

CONTENTS

Acknowledgements

The editor and publishers would like to thank:

A. D. Peters and Co Ltd and Harold Matson Company for 'R is for Rocket' by Ray Bradbury. First published in Great Britain in the anthology *R is for Rocket* by Rupert Hart-Davis Ltd 1968; copyright © 1943 Popular Productions Inc.

Laurence Pollinger Ltd for 'Skirmish' from *Strangers in the Universe* by Clifford Simak. This story copyright under the title 'Bathe your Bearings in Blood' © 1950 Ziff Davis Publishing Company.

Tony Richards for 'Rain' © Tony Richards 1985

Julia Birley for 'Come the Revolution!' © Julia Birley 1985

Charles E Fritch for 'No World for the Timid' from *Amazing Stories* © Charles E Fritch 1955

'Rain', 'Come the Revolution!' and 'The Waiting Game' are published for the first time in this collection.
Every effort has been made to trace the copyright holders of material used in this anthology. If notified of any omissions the publishers will be glad to make the proper corrections in future editions.

INTRODUCTION

In this fateful Orwellian year I'm writing to you on the fifteenth anniversary of Man's first landing on the moon. Many of you reading this will be too young to remember the dreamlike excitement so many of us felt, as we stayed up all night to watch those first few faltering steps, and the unforgettable words spoken by Neil Armstrong, quoted so often since but never again with that first sense of occasion: 'One small step for Man, one great leap for Mankind.'

Trite it may sound today, trite and obvious perhaps, but clichés aren't clichés when they are first coined. And sadly that giant step for Mankind has had to remain an isolated one. Despite space satellites, and the shuttle, the sense of spectacular achievement we felt as we watched events unfold on that memorable night, the real feeling of advancing into a new age, the Space Age, was never consolidated. As further moonshots came and went, public apathy took over. There was so much trouble on *this* world, too much, we were told, to justify the inordinate expense needed for Man's further interplanetary exploration. And anyway the information those first pioneers brought back could be gleaned quite as easily from unmanned vehicles which would not entail danger to human life.

One day things may be different. One day Man may land on Mars – perhaps in the lifetime of some of you who are reading this. Perhaps one day Man, having put his terrestrial house in order, may travel to the stars with a clear conscience. When earthly wars, famine and disease are conquered, interplanetary – even intergalactic – travel may become more than a dream.

Meanwhile we must confine our space travel to fiction, to reading about it in books like this; and if we cannot visit the planets, we can always speculate about what we would find if we could, and about the aliens who might one day decide to visit *our* planet.

Since the films *Close Encounters* and *ET*, hostile aliens have become unfashionable. We're now encouraged to assume that they'll be friendly. But excessive optimism is as rash as inordinate pessimism. When and if they come, they'll be no more likely to resemble Spielberg's cuddly ET than the Wellsian war machines. Probably the truth will lie somewhere between these two extremes. And maybe we won't know why they've come at all.

Personally I like my – fictional – aliens liberally tinged with menace.

A wise man once said that the monster you don't see is more effective in a story than the one you do. When the evil is revealed, the Unknown Terror is dissipated. In Tony Richards's *Rain*, the alien danger is revealed only to a select few. It is the physically blind who are signalled out for this dubious honour, and the story of *this* close encounter is a tensely effective antithesis to Wyndham's Triffid attack, where it is the handful of sighted survivors who are forearmed to confront the alien menace.

Captain Kirk and the crew of the Starship Enterprise are programmed, as every *Star Trek* fan knows, on no account to interfere or meddle with the culture and traditions of the alien societies which they meet – and this strict injunction is given to most fictional space travellers. When Vlad Massimo, one of the most unusual astronauts in the whole of space fiction, flouts this ruling, in Julia Birley's ingenious *Come the Revolution!* he almost causes the total destruction of life on Papillion.

The evolution of indigenous life-forms must be allowed to continue unimpeded, and this precept applies even to Earth.

When the threat to Frankenstein comes from the monster he has created, as it does in Clifford Simak's *Skirmish*, the resulting confrontation can be all the more bitter. This tale is comment on the first attempt of the servant race to oust the master (as, on the face of it, is Julia Birley's story) but this time it is machines that have developed their own awareness, and the first faint stirrings of the takeover bid are described in this wryly comic fantasy.

Whether it is ultimately the machine, or a hitherto unevolved organic species – a mutation perhaps – that will inherit the Earth, we won't know. Charles E Fritch, in *No World for the Timid* shows us just what might happen: a horrifying speculation for the future, in a world that is neither brave nor new, and certainly not for the timid, but polluted and corrupted beyond redemption. A grim story, and one for those who like their meat raw.

But in case you think that all is doom and gloom in *Space 9*, I have included a story from the Master himself – a story which never fails to move me, every time I read it. There are no aliens or ecological monsters or radioactive mutants in Ray Bradbury's *R is for Rocket*. Instead it celebrates the sheer joy and romance of space travel with a great flourish of trumpets. The two themes that constantly recur in Bradbury's work – nostalgia for childhood (specifically an American mid-Western boyhood) and the glamour of the rocketman, are here brought together in triumphant combination. Elsewhere Bradbury, like so many other SF writers, hasn't been slow to chart the dangers of rampant science unchecked – even on spaceships – but here all is sunny, positive and optimistic.

In a way *R is for Rocket* crystallizes and defines what so many of us felt on that day fifteen years ago when we heard Neil Armstrong's hopeful words, and we believed, albeit naïvely, that we were in truth entering a new era when people would work together in harmony, all earthly squabbles forgotten in a great adventure that would ultimately embrace the stars.

So to remind us that life isn't that easy, and that we must put away our rose-tinted spectacles, even if only temporarily, I have included a footnote by Rita Morris. *The Waiting Game* is set in Space. It is short, concise, and terribly apt, and it shows how one of the games we play on Earth might tragically survive the very Earth itself.

As with all the other volumes in this series I have tried to present as varied a menu as possible. I hope the stories will entertain you: and I hope that at the same time they will give you something to think about.

But most of all I hope you enjoy them.

RICHARD DAVIS
Blandford Forum, Dorset, 1984

R IS FOR ROCKET

Ray Bradbury

There was this fence where we pressed our faces and felt the wind turn warm and held to the fence and forgot who we were or where we came from but dreamed of who we might be and where we might go . . . .

Yet we were boys and liked being boys and lived in a Florida town and liked the town and went to school and fairly liked the school and climbed trees and played football and liked our mothers and fathers . . . .

But some time every hour of every day of every week for a minute or a second when we thought on fire and stars and the fence beyond which they waited . . . we liked the rockets more.

The fence. The rockets.

Every Saturday morning . . . .

The guys met at my house.

With the sun hardly up, they yelled until the neighbours were moved to brandish paralysis guns out their ventilators commanding the guys to shut up or they'd be frozen statues for the next hour and *then* where would they be?

Aw, climb a rocket, stick your head in the main-jet! the kids always yelled back, but yelled this safe behind our garden fence. Old Man Wickard, next door, is a great shot with the para-gun.

This one dim cool Saturday morning I was lying in bed thinking about how I had flunked my semantics exam the day before at formula-school, when I heard the gang yelling below. It was hardly 7 a.m. and there was still a lot of fog roaming in off the Atlantic, and only now were the weather-control vibrators at each corner starting to hum and shoot out rays to get rid of the stuff; I heard them moaning soft and nice.

I padded to the window and stuck my head out.

'Okay, space-pirates! Motors off!'

'Hey!' shouted Ralph Priory. 'We just heard, there's a new schedule today! The Moon Job, the one with the new XL3-motor, is cutting gravity in an *hour*!'

'Buddha, Muhammad, Allah, and other real and semi-mythological figures,' I said, and went away from the window so fast the concussion laid all the boys out on my lawn.

I zippered myself into a jumper, yanked on my boots, clipped my food-capsules to my hip-pocket, for I knew there'd be no food or even thought of food today, we'd just stuff with pills when our stomachs barked, and fell down the two-storey vacuum elevator.

On the lawn, all five of the guys were chewing their lips, bouncing around, scowling.

'Last one,' said I, passing them at five thousand miles per hour, 'to the monorail is a bug-eyed Martian!'

On the monorail, with the cylinder hissing us along to Rocket Port, twenty miles from town – a few minutes' ride – I had bugs in my stomach. A guy fifteen doesn't get to see the big stuff often enough, mostly every week it was the small continental cargo rockets coming and going on schedule. But this was big, among the biggest ... the Moon and beyond. . . .

'I'm sick,' said Priory, and hit me on the arm.

I hit him back. 'Me, too. Boy, ain't Saturday the best day in the week!?'

Priory and I traded wide, understanding grins. We got along all Condition Go. The other pirates were okay. Sid Rossen, Mac Leslyn, Earl Marnee, they knew how to jump around like all the kids, and they loved the rockets too, but I had the feeling they wouldn't be doing what Ralph and I would do some day. Ralph and I wanted the stars for each of us, more than we would want a fistful of clear-cut blue-white diamonds.

We yelled with the yellers, we laughed with the laughers, but at the middle of it all, we were still, Ralph and I, and the cylinder whispered to a stop and we were outside yelling, laughing, running, but quiet and almost in slow motion, Ralph ahead of me, and all of us pointed one way, at the observation fence and grabbing hold, yelling for the slow-pokes to catch up, but not looking back for them, and then we were all there together and the big rocket came out of its plastic work canopy like a great interstellar circus tent and moved along its gleaming track out towards the fire point, accompanied by the gigantic gantry like a gathering of pre-historic reptile birds which kept and preened and fed this one big fire monster and led it towards its seizure and birth into a suddenly blast-furnace sky.

I quit breathing. I didn't even suck another breath it seemed until the rocket was way out on the concrete meadow, followed by water-beetle tractors and great cylinders bearing hidden men, and all around, in asbestos suits, praying-mantis mechanics fiddled with machines and buzzed and cawwed and gibbered to each other on invisible, unhearable radiophones, but we could hear it all, in our heads, our minds, our hearts.

'Lord,' I said at last.

'The very good Lord,' said Ralph Priory at my elbow.

The others said this, too, over and over.

It was something to 'good Lord' about. It was a hundred years of dreaming all sorted out and chosen and put together to make the hardest, prettiest, swiftest dream of all. Every line was fire solidified and made perfect, it was flame frozen, and ice waiting to thaw there in the middle of a concrete prairie, ready to wake with a roar, jump high and knock its silly fine great head against the Milky Way and knock the stars down in a full return of fireball meteors. You felt it could kick the Coal Sack Nebula square in the midriff and make it stand out of the way.

It got me in the midriff, too – it gripped me in such a way I knew the special sickness of longing and envy and grief for lack of accomplishment. And when the astronauts patrolled the field in the final silent mobile-van, my body went with them in their strange white armour, in their bubble-helmets and insouciant pride, looking as if they were team-parading to a magnetic football game at one of the local mag-fields, for mere practice. But they were going to the Moon, they went every month now, and the crowds that used to come to watch were no longer there, there was just us kids to worry them up and worry them off.

'Gosh,' I said. 'What wouldn't I give to go with them. What wouldn't I give.'

'Me,' said Mac, 'I'd give my one-year monorail privileges.'

'Yeah. Oh, very much yeah.'

It was a big feeling for us kids, caught half between this morning's toys and this afternoon's very real and powerful fireworks.

And then the preliminaries got over with. The fuel was in the rocket and the men ran away from it on the ground like ants running lickety from a metal god – and the Dream woke up and gave a yell and jumped into the sky. And then it was gone, all the vacuum-shouting of it, leaving nothing but a hot trembling in the air, through the ground, and up our legs to our hearts. Where it had been was a blazed, seared pock and a fog of rocket smoke like a cumulus cloud banked low.

'It's gone!' yelled Priory.

And we all began to breathe fast again, frozen there on the

ground as if stunned by the passing of a gigantic paralysis gun.

'I want to grow up quick,' I said, then. 'I want to grow up quick so I can take that rocket.'

I bit my lips. I was so darned young, and you cannot apply for space work. You have to be *chosen*. Chosen.

Finally somebody, I guess it was Sidney, said: 'Let's go to the tele-show now.'

Everyone said yeah, except Priory and myself. We said no, and the other kids went off laughing breathlessly, talking, and left Priory and me there to look at the spot where the ship had been.

It spoiled everything else for us – that take off.

Because of it, I flunked my semantics test on Monday. I didn't care.

At times like that I thanked Providence for concentrates. When your stomach is nothing but a coiled mass of excitement, you hardly feel like drawing a chair to a full hot dinner. A few concen-tabs swallowed, did wonderfully well as substitution, without the urge of appetite.

I got to thinking about it, tough and hard, all day long and late at night. It got so bad I had to use sleep-massage mechs every night, coupled with some of Tschaikovsky's quieter music to get my eyes shut.

'Good Lord, young man,' said my teacher, that Monday at class. 'If this keeps up I'll have you reclassified at the next psych-board meeting.'

'I'm sorry,' I replied.

He looked hard at me. 'What sort of block have you got? It must be a very simple, and also a conscious, one.'

I winced. 'It's conscious, sir; but it's not simple. It's multi-tentacular. In brief, though – it's rockets.'

He smiled. 'R is for Rocket, eh?'

'I guess that's it, sir.'

'We can't let it interfere with your scholastic record, though, young man.'

'Do you think I need hypnotic suggestion, sir?'

'No, no.' He flipped through a small tab of records with my name blocked on it. I had a funny stone in my stomach, just lying there. He looked at me. 'You know, Christopher, you're king-of-the-hill here; head of the class.' He closed his eyes and mused over it. 'We'll have to see about a lot of other things,' he concluded. Then he patted me on the shoulder.

'Well – get on with your work. Nothing to worry about.'

He walked away.

I tried to get back to work, but I couldn't. During the rest of the day the teacher kept watching me and looking at my tab-record and chewing his lip. About two in the afternoon he dialled a number on his desk-audio and discussed something with somebody for about five minutes.

I couldn't hear what was said.

But when he set the audio into its cradle, he stared straight at me with the funniest light in his eyes.

It was envy and admiration and pity all in one. It was a little sad and it was much of happiness. It had a lot in it, just in his eyes. The rest of his face said nothing.

It made me feel like a saint and a devil sitting there.

Ralph Priory and I slid home from formula-school together early that afternoon. I told Ralph what had happened and he frowned in the dark way he always frowns.

I began to worry. And between the two of us we doubled and tripled the worry.

'You don't think you'll be sent away, do you, Chris?'

Our monorail car hissed. We stopped at our station. We got out. We walked slow. 'I don't know,' I said.

'That would be plain dirty,' said Ralph.

'Maybe I need a good psychiatric laundering, Ralph. I can't go on flubbing my studies this way.'

We stopped outside my house and looked at the sky for a long moment. Ralph said something funny.

'The stars aren't out in the daytime, but we can see 'em,

can't we, Chris?'

'Yeah,' I said. 'Darn right.'

'We'll stick it together, huh, Chris? Blast them, they can't take you away now. We're pals. It wouldn't be fair.'

I didn't say anything because there was no room in my throat for anything but a hectagonal lump.

'What's the matter with your eyes?' asked Priory.

'Aw, I looked at the sun too long. Come on inside, Ralph.'

We yelled under the shower spray in the bath-cubicle, but our yells weren't especially convincing, even when we turned on the ice-water.

While we were standing in the warm-air dryer, I did a lot of thinking. Literature, I figured, was full of people who fought battles against hard, razor-edged opponents. They pitted brain and muscle against obstacles until they won out or were themselves defeated. But here I was with hardly a sign of any outward conflict. It was all running around in spiked boots inside my head, making cuts and bruises where no one could see them except me and a psychologist. But it was just as bad.

'Ralph,' I said, as we dressed, 'I got a war on.'

'All by yourself?' he asked.

'I can't include you,' I said, 'because this is personal. How many times has my mother said, "Don't eat so much, Chris, your eyes are bigger than your stomach"?'

'A million times.'

'*Two* million. Well, paraphrase it, Ralph. Change it to "Don't *see* so much, Chris, your mind is too big for your body". I got a war on between a mind that wants things my body can't give it.'

Priory nodded quietly. 'I see what you mean about its being a personal war. In that case, Christopher, I'm at war, too.'

'I knew you were,' I said. 'Somehow I think the other kids'll grow out of it. But I don't think we will, Ralph. I think we'll keep waiting.'

17

We sat down in the middle of the sunlit upper deck of the house, and started checking over some homework on our formula-pads. Priory couldn't get his. Neither could I. Priory put into words the very thing I didn't dare say out loud. 'Chris, the Astronaut Board *selects*. You can't apply for it. You *wait*.'

'I know.'

'You wait from the time you're old enough to turn cold in the stomach when you see a Moon rocket, until all the years go by, and every month that passes you hope that one morning a blue Astronaut helicopter will come down out of the sky, land on your lawn, and that a neat-looking engineer will ease out, walk up the rampway briskly, and touch the bell.

'You keep waiting for that helicopter until you're twenty-one. And then, on the last day of your twentieth year you drink and laugh a lot and say what the heck, you didn't really care about it, anyway.'

We both just sat there, deep in the middle of his words. We both just sat there. Then:

'I don't want that disappointment, Chris. I'm fifteen, just like you. But if I reach my twenty-first year without an Astronaut ringing the bell where I live at the ortho-station, I—'

'I know,' I said. 'I know. I've talked to men who've waited, all for nothing. And if it happens that way to us, Ralph, well – we'll get good and drunk together and then go out and take jobs loading cargo on a Europe-bound freighter.'

Ralph stiffened and his face went pale. 'Loading cargo.'

There was a soft, quick step on the ramp and my mother was there. I smiled. 'Hi, lady!'

'Hello. Hello, Ralph.'

'Hello, Jhene.'

She didn't look much older than twenty-five, in spite of having birthed and raised me and worked at the Government Statistics House. She was light and graceful and smiled

18

a lot, and I could see how father must have loved her very much when he was alive. One parent is better than none. Poor Priory, now, raised in one of those orthopaedical stations . . . .

Jhene walked over and put her hand on Ralph's face. 'You look ill,' she said. 'What's wrong?'

Ralph managed a fairly good smile. 'Nothing – at all.'

Jhene didn't need prompting. She said, 'You can stay here tonight, Priory. We want you. Don't we, Chris?'

'Heck, yes.'

'I should get back to the station,' said Ralph, rather feebly, I observed. 'But since you asked and Chris here needs help on his semantics for tomorrow, I'll stick and help him.'

'Very generous,' I observed.

'First, though, I've a few errands. I'll take the 'rail and be back in an hour, people.'

When Ralph was gone my mother looked at me intently, then brushed my hair back with a nice little move of her fingers.

'Something's happening, Chris.'

My heart stopped talking because it didn't want to talk any more for a while. It waited.

I opened my mouth, but Jhene went on:

'Something's up somewhere. I had two calls at work today. One from your teacher. One from – I can't say. I don't *want* to say until things happen—'

My heart started talking again, slow and warm.

'Don't tell me, then, Jhene. Those calls—'

She just looked at me. She took my hand between her two soft warm ones. 'You're so young, Chris. You're so awfully young.'

I didn't speak.

Her eyes brightened. 'You never knew your father. I wish you had. You know what he was, Chris?'

I said, 'Yeah. He worked in a Chemistry Lab, deep underground most of the time.'

And my mother added, strangely, 'He worked deep under

the ground, Chris, and never saw the stars.'

My heart yelled in my chest. Yelled loud and hard.

'Oh, Mother. Mother—'

It was the first time in years I had called her mother.

When I woke the next morning there was a lot of sunlight in the room, but the cushion where Priory slept when he stayed over was vacant. I listened. I didn't hear him splashing in the shower-cube, and the dryer wasn't humming. He was gone.

I found his note pinned on the sliding door.

> 'See you at formula at noon. Your mother wanted me to do some work for her. She got a call this morning, and said she needed me to help. So long. Priory.'

Priory out running errands for Jhene. Strange. A call in the early morning to Jhene. I went back and sat down on the cushion.

While I was sitting there a bunch of the kids yelled down on the lawn-court. 'Hey, Chris! You're late!'

I stuck my head out of the window. 'Be right down!'

'No, Chris.'

My mother's voice. It was quiet and it had something funny in it. I turned around. She was standing in the doorway behind me, her face pale, drawn, full of some small pain. 'No, Chris,' she said again, softly. 'Tell them to go on to formula without you – today.'

The kids were still making noise downstairs, I guess, but I didn't hear them. I just felt myself and my mother, slim and pale and restrained in my room. Far off, the weather-control vibrators started to hum and throb.

I turned slowly and looked down at the kids. The three of them were looking up, lips parted casually, half-smiling, semantic-tabs in their knotty fingers. 'Hey—' one of them said. Sidney, it was.

'Sorry, Sid. Sorry, gang. Go on without me. I can't go to formula today. See you later, huh?'

'Aw, Chris!'

'Sick?'

'No. Just— Just go on without me, gang. I'll see you.'

I felt numb. I turned away from their upturned, question-
ing faces and glanced at the door. Mother wasn't there. She
had gone downstairs, quietly. I heard the kids moving off,
not quite as boisterously, towards the monorail station.

Instead of using the vac-elevator, I walked slowly
downstairs. 'Jhene,' I said, 'where's Ralph?'

Jhene pretended to be interested in combing her long light
hair with a vibro-toothed comb. 'I sent him off. I didn't want
him here this morning.'

'Why am I staying home from formula, Jhene?'

'Chris, please don't ask.'

Before I could say anything else, there was a sound in the
air. It cut through the very soundproofed wall of the house,
and hummed in my marrow, quick and high as an arrow of
glittering music.

I swallowed. All the fear and uncertainty and doubt went
away, instantly.

When I heard that note, I thought of Ralph Priory. *Oh,
Ralph, if you could be here now.* I couldn't believe the truth of it.
Hearing that note and hearing it with my whole body and
soul as well as with my ears.

It came closer, that sound. I was afraid it would go away.
But it didn't go away. It lowered its pitch and came down outside the house in great whirling petals of light and shadow
and I knew it was a helicopter the colour of the sky. It
stopped humming, and in the silence my mother tensed for-
ward, dropped the vibro-comb and took in her breath.

In that silence, too, I heard booted footsteps walking up
the ramp below. Footsteps that I had waited for, for a long
time.

Footsteps I was afraid would never come.

Somebody touched the bell.

And I *knew* who it was.

And all I could think was, Ralph, why in heck did you have

21

to go away now, when all this is happening? Blast it, Ralph, why did you?

The man looked as if he had been born in his uniform. It fitted like a second layer of salt-coloured skin, touched here and there with a line, a dot of blue. As simple and perfect a uniform as could be made, but with all the muscled power of the universe behind it.

His name was Trent. He spoke firmly, with a natural round perfection, directly to the subject.

I stood there, and my mother was on the far side of the room, looking like a bewildered little girl. I stood listening.

Out of all the talking I remember some of the snatches:

'. . . highest grades, high IQ. Perception A-1, curiosity Triple-A. Enthusiasm necessary to the long, eight-year educational grind . . . .'

'Yes, sir.'

'. . . talks with your semantics and psychology teachers—'

'Yes, sir.'

'. . . and don't forget, Mr Christopher . . .'

Mister Christopher!

'. . . and don't forget, Mr Christopher, nobody is to know you have been selected by the Astronaut Board.'

'No one?'

'Your mother and teacher know, naturally. But no other person must know. Is that perfectly understood?'

'Yes, sir.'

Trent smiled quietly, standing there with his big hands at his sides. 'You want to ask why, don't you? Why you can't tell your friends? I'll explain.

'It's a form of psychological protection. We select about ten thousand young men each year from the earth's billions. Out of that number three thousand wind up, eight years later, as spacemen of one sort of another. The others must return to society. They've flunked out, but there's no reason for everyone to know. They usually flunk out, if they're going to flunk, in the first six months. And it's tough to go back and face your friends and say you couldn't make the grade at the biggest job in the world. So we make it easy to go back. 'But there's still another reason. It's psychological, too. Half the fun of being a kid is being able to lord it over the other guys, by being superior in some way. We take half the fun out of Astronaut selection by strictly forbidding you to tell your pals. Then, we'll know if you wanted to go into space for frivolous reasons, or for space itself. If you're in it for personal conceit – you're damned. If you're in it because you can't help being in it and *have* to be in it – you're blessed.'

He nodded to my mother. 'Thank you, Mrs Christopher.'

'Sir,' I said. 'A question. I have a friend. Ralph Priory. He lives at an ortho-station—'

Trent nodded. 'I can't tell you his rating, of course, but he's on our list. He's your buddy? You want him along, of course. I'll check his record. Station-bred, you say? That's not good. But – we'll see.'

'If you would, please, thanks.'

'Report to me at the Rocket Station Saturday afternoon at five, Mr Christopher. Meantime: silence.'

He saluted. He walked off. He went away in the helicopter into the sky, and Mother was beside me quickly, saying, 'Oh, Chris, Chris,' over and over, and we held to each other and whispered and talked and she said many things, how good this was going to be for us, but especially for me, how fine, what an honour it was, like the old old days when men fasted and took vows and joined churches and stopped up their tongues and were silent and prayed to be worthy and to live well as monks and priests of many churches in far places, and came forth and moved in the world and lived as examples and taught well. It was no different now, this was a greater priesthood, in a way, she said, she inferred, she knew, and I was to be some small part of it, I would not be hers any more, I would belong to all the worlds, I would be all the things my father wanted to be and never lived or had a chance to be . . . .

'Darn right, darn right, I murmured. 'I will, I promise I will . . .'

I caught my voice. 'Jhene – how – how will we tell Ralph? What about him?'

'You're going away, that's all, Chris. Tell him that. Very simply. Tell him no more. He'll understand.'

'But, Jhene, *you—*'

She smiled softly. 'Yes, I'll be lonely, Chris. But I'll have my work and I'll have Ralph.'

'You mean –'

'I'm taking him from the ortho-station. He'll live here, when you're gone. That's what you *wanted* me to say, isn't it, Chris?'

I nodded, all paralysed and strange inside.

'That's exactly what I wanted you to say.'

'He'll be a good son, Chris. *Almost* as good as you.'

'He'll be *fine!*'

We told Ralph Priory. How I was going away maybe to school in Europe for a year and how Mother wanted him to come live as her son, now, until such time as I came back. We said it quick and fast, as if it burned our tongues. And when we finished, Ralph came and shook my hand and kissed my mother on the cheek and he said:

'I'll be proud. I'll be very proud.'

It was funny, but Ralph didn't even ask any more about why I was going, or where, or how long I would be away. All he would say was, 'We had a lot of fun, didn't we?' and let it go at that, as if he didn't dare say any more.

It was Friday night, after a concert at the amphitheatre in the centre of our public circle, and Priory and Jhene and I came home, laughing, ready to go to bed.

I hadn't packed anything. Priory noted this briefly, and let it go. All of my personal supplies for the next eight years would be supplied by someone else. No need for packing.

My semantics teacher called on the audio, smiling and saying a very brief, pleasant goodbye.

Then we went to bed, and I kept thinking in the hour before I lolled off, about how this was the last night with Jhene and Ralph. The very last night.

Only a kid of fifteen – me.

And then, in the darkness, just before I went to sleep, Priory twisted softly on his cushion, turned his solemn face to me, and whispered, 'Chris?' A pause. 'Chris. You still awake?' It was like a faint echo.

'Yes,' I said.

'Thinking?'

A pause.

'Yes.'

He said, 'You're— You're not *waiting* any more, are you, Chris?'

I knew what he meant. I couldn't answer.

I said, 'I'm awfully tired, Ralph.'

He twisted back and settled down and said, 'That's what I thought. You're not *waiting* any more. Gosh, but that's good, Chris. That's good.'

He reached out and punched me in the arm-muscle, lightly.

Then we both went to sleep.

It was Saturday morning. The kids were yelling outside. Their voices filled the seven o'clock fog. I heard Old Man Wickard's ventilator flip open and the zip of his para-gun, playfully touching around the kids.

'Shut up!' I heard him cry, but he didn't sound grouchy. It was a regular Saturday game with him. And I heard the kids giggle.

Priory woke up and said, 'Shall I tell them, Chris, you're not going with them today?'

'Tell them nothing of the sort.' Jhene moved from the door. She bent out the window, her hair all light against a ribbon of fog. 'Hi, gang! Ralph and Chris will be right down. Hold gravity!'

'Jhene!' I cried.

She came over to both of us. 'You're going to spend your Saturday the way you always spend it – with the gang!'

'I planned on sticking with you, Jhene.'

'What sort of holiday would *that* be, now?'

She ran us through our breakfast, kissed us on the cheeks, and forced us out the door into the gang's arms.

'Let's not go out to the Rocket Port today, guys.'

'Aw, Chris – why not?'

Their faces did a lot of changes. This was the first time in history I hadn't wanted to go. 'You're kidding, Chris.'

'Sure he is.'

'No, he's not. He means it,' said Priory. 'And I don't want to go either. We go *every* Saturday. It gets tiresome. We can go next week instead.'

'Aw . . . .'

They didn't like it, but they didn't go off by themselves. It was no fun, they said, without us.

'What the heck – we'll go next week.'

'Sure we will. What do you want to do, Chris?'

I told them.

We spent the morning playing kick-the-can and some games we'd given up a long time ago, and we hiked out along some old rusty and abandoned railway tracks and walked in a small woods outside town and photographed some birds and went swimming raw, and all the time I kept thinking – this is the last day.

We did everything we had ever done before on Saturday. All the silly crazy things, and nobody knew I was going away except Ralph, and five o'clock kept getting nearer and nearer.

At four, I said goodbye to the kids.

'Leaving so soon, Chris? What about tonight?'

'Call for me at eight,' I said. 'We'll go see the new Sally Gibberts picture!'

26

'Swell.'

'Cut gravity!'

And Ralph and I went home.

Mother wasn't there, but she had left part of herself, her smile and her voice and her words on a spool of audio-film on my bed. I inserted it in the viewer and threw the picture on the wall. Soft yellow hair, her white face and her quiet words:

'I hate goodbyes, Chris. I've gone to the laboratory to do some extra work. Good luck. All of my love. When I see you again – you'll be a man.'

That was all.

Priory waited outside while I saw it over four times. 'I hate goodbyes, Chris. I've gone . . . work . . . luck. All . . . my love . . . .'

I had made a film-spool myself the night before. I spotted it in the viewer and left it there. It only said goodbye.

Priory walked halfway with me. I wouldn't let him get on the Rocket Port monorail with me. I just shook his hand, tight, and said, 'It was fun today, Ralph.'

'Yeah. Well see you next Saturday, huh, Chris?'

'I wish I could say yes.'

'Say yes anyway. Next Saturday – the woods, the gang, the rockets, and Old Man Wickard and his trusty para-gun.'

We laughed. 'Sure. Next Saturday, early. Take— Take care of *our* mother, will you, Priory?'

'That's a silly question, you nut,' he said.

'It is, isn't it?'

He swallowed. 'Chris.'

'Yeah.'

'I'll be waiting. Just like you waited and don't have to wait any more. I'll *wait*.'

'Maybe it won't be long, Priory. I hope not.'

I jabbed him, once, in the arm. He jabbed back.

The monorail door sealed. The car hurled itself away, and Priory was left behind.

I stepped out at the Port. It was a five-hundred-yard walk

down to the Administration building. It took me ten years to walk it.

'Next time I see you you'll be a man—'

'Don't tell anybody—'

'I'll wait, Chris—'

It was all choked in my heart and it wouldn't go away and it swam around in my eyes.

I thought about my dreams. The Moon Rocket. It won't be part of me, part of my *dream* any longer. I'll be part of *it*.

I felt small there, walking, walking, walking.

The afternoon rocket to London was just taking off as I went down the ramp to the office. It shivered the ground and it shivered and thrilled my heart.

I was beginning to grow up awfully fast.

I stood watching the rocket until someone snapped their heels, cracked me a quick salute.

I was numb.

'C. M. Christopher?'

'Yes, sir. Reporting, sir.'

'This way, Christopher. Through that gate.'

Through that gate and beyond *the* fence . . . .

This fence where we had pressed our faces and felt the wind turn warm and held to the fence and forgot who we were or where we came from but dreamed of who we might be and where we might go . . . .

This fence where had stood the boys who liked being boys who lived in a town and liked the town and fairly liked school and liked football and liked their fathers and mothers . . . .

The boys who some time every hour of every day of every week thought on fire and stars and the fence beyond which they waited . . . . The boys who liked the rockets *more*.

Mother, Ralph, I'll see you. I'll be back.

Mother!

Ralph!

And, walking, I went beyond the fence.

SKIRMISH

Clifford Simak

It was a good watch. It had been a good watch for more than thirty years. His father had owned it first, and his mother had saved if for him after his father died and had given it to him on his eighteenth birthday. For all the years since then it had served him faithfully.

But now, comparing it with the clock on the newsroom wall, looking from his wrist to the big face of the clock over the coat cabinets, Joe Crane was forced to admit that his watch was wrong. It was an hour fast. His watch said seven o'clock and the clock on the wall insisted it was only six.

Come to think of it, it had seemed unusually dark driving down to work, and the streets had appeared singularly deserted.

He stood quietly in the empty newsroom, listening to the muttering of the row of teletype machines. Overhead lights shone here and there, gleaming on waiting telephones, on typewriters, on the china whiteness of the pastepots huddled in a group on the copy desk.

Quiet now, he thought, quiet and peace and shadow, but

in another hour the place would spring to life. Ed Lane, the news editor, would arrive at six-thirty, and shortly after that Frank McKay, the city editor, would come lumbering in.

Crane put up a hand and rubbed his eyes. He could have used that extra hour of sleep. He could have—

Wait a minute! He had not got up by the watch upon his wrist. The alarm clock had awakened him. And that meant the alarm clock was an hour fast, too.

'It don't make sense,' said Crane aloud.

He shuffled past the copy desk, heading for his chair and typewriter. Something moved on the desk alongside the typewriter – a thing that glinted, rat-sized and shiny and with a certain indefinable manner about it that made him stop short in his tracks with a sense of gulping emptiness in his throat and belly.

The thing squatted by the typewriter and stared across the room at him. There was no sign of eyes, no hint of face, and yet he knew it stared.

Acting almost instinctively, Crane reached out and grabbed a pastepot off the copy desk. He hurled it with a vicious motion and it became a white blur in the lamplight, spinning end over end. It caught the staring thing squarely, lifted it, and swept it off the desk. The pastepot hit the floor and broke, scattering broken shards and oozy gobs of half-dried paste.

The shining thing hit the floor somersaulting. Its feet made metallic sounds as it righted itself and dashed across the floor.

Crane's hand scooped up a spike, heavily weighted with metal. He threw it with a sudden gush of hatred and revulsion. The spike hit the floor with a thud ahead of the running thing and drove its point deep into the wood.

The metal rat made splinters fly as it changed its course. Desperately it flung itself through the three-inch opening of a supply cabinet door.

Crane sprinted swiftly, hit the door with both hands, and slammed it shut.

30

'Got you,' he said.

He thought about it, standing with his back against the door.

Scared, he thought. Scared silly by a shining thing that looked something like a rat. Maybe it *was* a rat, a white rat.

And yet, it hadn't had a tail. It didn't have a face. Yet it had looked at him.

Crazy, he said. Crane, you're going nuts.

It didn't quite make sense. It didn't fit into this morning of 18 October 1962. Nor into the twentieth century. Nor into normal human life.

He turned around, grasped the doorknob firmly and wrenched, intending to throw it wide open in one sudden jerk. But the knob slid beneath his fingers and would not move, and the door stayed shut.

Locked, thought Crane. The lock snapped home when I slammed the door. And I haven't got the key. Dorothy Graham has the key, but she always leaves the door open because it's hard to get it open once it's locked. She almost always has to call one of the janitors. Maybe there's some of the maintenance men around. Maybe I should hunt one up and tell him—

Tell him what? Tell him I saw a metal rat run into the cabinet? Tell him I threw a pastepot at it and knocked it off the desk? That I threw a spike at it, too, and to prove it, there's the spike sticking in the floor?

Crane shook his head.

He walked over to the spike and yanked it from the floor. He put the spike back on the copy desk and kicked the fragments of the pastepot out of sight.

At his own desk, he selected three sheets of paper and rolled them into the typewriter.

The machine started to type. All by itself without his touching it! He sat stupified and watched its keys go up and down. It typed: *Keep out of this, Joe, don't mix into this. You might get hurt.*

Joe Crane pulled the sheets of copy paper out of the machine. He balled them in his fist and threw them into a waste-basket. Then he went out to get a cup of coffee.

'You know, Louie,' he said to the man behind the counter, 'a man lives alone too long and he gets to seeing things.'

'Yeah,' said Louie. 'Me, I'd go nuts in that place of yours. Rattling around in it empty-like. Should have sold it when your old lady passed on.'

'Couldn't,' said Crane. 'It's been my home too long.'

'Ought to get married off, then,' said Louie. 'Ain't good to live by yourself.'

'Too late now.' Crane told him. 'There isn't anyone who would put up with me.'

'You been seeing things?' asked Louie abruptly.

'Seeing things?'

'Yeah. You said a man lives too much alone and he gets to seeing things.'

'Just a figure of speech,' said Crane.

He finished the cup of coffee quickly and went back to the office.

The place looked more familiar now. Ed Lane was there, cussing out a copy boy. Frank McKay was clipping the opposition morning sheet. A couple of other reporters had drifted in.

Crane took a quick look at the supply cabinet door. It was still shut.

The phone on McKay's desk buzzed and the city editor picked it up. He listened for a moment, then took it down from his ear and held his hand over the mouthpiece.

'Joe,' he said, 'take this. Some screwball claims he met a sewing machine coming down the street.'

Crane reached for his phone. 'Give me the call on 245,' he told the operator.

A voice was saying in his ear, 'This is the *Herald*? This is the *Herald*? Hello, there . . . .'

'This is Crane,' said Joe.

'I want the *Herald*,' said the man. 'I want to tell 'em . . . .'

'This is Crane of the *Herald*,' Crane told him. 'What's on your mind?'

'You a reporter?'

'Yeah, I'm a reporter.'

'Then listen close. I'll try to tell this slow and easy and just the way it happened. I was walking down the street, see, when . . . .'

'What street?' asked Crane. 'And what is your name?'

'East Lake,' said the caller. 'The five- or six-hundred block. I don't remember which. And I met this sewing machine rolling along the street and I thought, thinking the way you would, you know, if you met a sewing machine – I thought somebody had been rolling it along and it had gotten away from them. Although that is funny, because the street is level. There's no grade to it at all, you see. Sure, you know the place. Level as the palm of your hand. And there wasn't a soul in sight. It was early morning, see . . . .'

'What's your name?' asked Crane.

'My name? Smith, that's my name. Jeff Smith. And so I figured maybe I'd ought to help this guy the sewing machine had gotten away from, so I put out my hand to stop it and it dodged. It—'

'It did what?' yelped Crane.

'It dodged. So help me, mister. When I put my hand out to stop it, it dodged out of the way so I couldn't catch it. As if it knew I was trying to catch it, see, and it didn't want to be caught. So it dodged out of the way and went around me and down the street as fast as it could go, picking up speed as it went. And when it got to the corner, it turned the corner as slick as you please, and—'

'What's your address?' asked Crane.

'My address? Say, what do you want my address for; I was telling you about this sewing machine. I called you up to give you a story and you keep interrupting—'

'I've got to have your address,' Crane told him, 'if I'm going to write the story.'

'Oh, all right then, if that's the way it is. I live at 203 North

Hampton and I work at Axel Machines. Run a lathe, you know. And I haven't had a drink in weeks. I'm cold sober now.'

'All right,' said Crane. 'Go ahead and tell me.'

'Well, there isn't much else to tell. Only when this machine went past me I had the funny feeling that it was watching me. Out of the corner of its eyes, kind of. And how is a sewing machine going to watch you; a sewing machine hasn't got any eyes and . . . .'

'What made you think it was watching you?'

'I don't know, mister. Just a feeling. Like my skin was trying to roll up my back.'

'Mr Smith,' asked Crane, 'have you ever seen a thing like this before? Say, a washing machine, or something else?'

'I ain't drunk,' said Smith, 'if *that's* what you mean – haven't had a drop in weeks. I never saw nothing like this before. But I'm telling you the truth, mister. I got a good reputation. You can call up anyone and ask them. Call Johnny Jacobson up at the Red Rooster grocery. He knows me. He can tell you about me. He can tell you—'

'Sure, sure,' said Crane, pacifying him. 'Thanks for calling, Mr Smith.'

You and a guy named Smith, he told himself. Both of you are nuts. You saw a metal rat and your typewriter talked back at you, and now this guy meets a sewing machine strolling down the street.

Dorothy Graham, the managing editor's secretary, went past his desk, walking rapidly, her high heels coming down with decisive clicks. Her face was flushed an angry pink and she was jingling a ring of keys in her hands.

'What's the matter, Dorothy?' Crane asked.

'It's that damn door again,' she said. 'The one to the supply cabinet. I just know I left it open and now some goof comes along and closes it and the lock snaps.'

'Keys won't open it?' asked Crane.

'Nothing will open it,' she snapped. 'Now I've got to get George up here again. He knows how to do it. Talks to it or something. It makes me so mad – Boss called up last night and said for me to be down early and get the wire recorder for Albertson. He's going out on that murder trial up north and wants to get some of the stuff down on tape. So I get up early, and what does it get me? I lose my sleep and don't even stop for breakfast and now . . . .'

'Get an axe,' said Crane. 'That will open it.'

'The worst of it,' said Dorothy, 'is that George never gets the lead out. He always says he'll be right up and then I wait and wait and I call again and he says—'

'Crane!' McKay's roar echoed through the room.

'Yeah,' said Crane.

'Anything to that sewing machine story?'

'Guy says he met one.'

'Anything to it?'

'How the hell would I know? I got the guy's word, that's all.'

'Well, call up some other people down in that neighbourhood. Ask them if they saw a sewing machine running around loose. Might be good for a humorous piece.'

'Sure,' said Crane.

He could imagine it:

'This is Crane at the *Herald*. Got a report there's a sewing machine running around loose down in your neighbourhood. Wondering if you saw anything of it. Yes, lady, that's what I said . . . a sewing machine running around. No, ma'am, no one was pushing it. Just running around . . . .'

He slouched out of his chair, went over to the reference table, picked up the city directory, and lugged it back to the desk. Doggedly he opened the book, located the East Lake listings, and made some notes of names and addresses. He dawdled, reluctant to start phoning. He walked to the window and looked out at the weather. He wished he didn't have to work. He thought of the kitchen sink at home. Plugged up again. He'd taken it apart, and there were couplings and pipes and union joints spread all over the place. Today, he thought, would be a nice day to fix that sink.

When he went back to the desk, McKay came and stood over him.

'What do you think of it, Joe?'

'Screwball,' said Crane, hoping McKay would call it off.

'Good feature story, though,' said the editor. 'Have some fun with it.'

'Sure,' said Crane.

McKay left and Crane made some calls. He got the sort of reaction that he expected.

He started to write the story. It didn't go so well. *A sewing machine went for a stroll down Lake Street this morning . . . .* He ripped out the sheet and threw it in the waste-basket.

He dawdled some more, then wrote: *A man met a sewing machine rolling down Lake Street this morning and the man lifted his hat most politely and said to the sewing machine . . . .* He ripped out the sheet.

He tried again: *Can a sewing machine walk? That is, can it go for a walk without someone pushing it or pulling it or . . . .* He tore out the sheet, inserted a new one, then got up and started for the water fountain to get a drink.

'Getting something, Joe?' McKay asked.

'Have it for you in a while,' said Crane.

He stopped at the picture desk and Gattard, the picture editor, handed him the morning's offerings.

'Nothing much to pep you up,' said Gattard. 'All the gals got a bad dose of modesty today.'

Crane looked through the sheaf of pictures. There wasn't, truth to tell, so much feminine epidermis as usual, although the gal who was Miss Manilla Rope wasn't bad at all.

'The place is going to go to hell,' mourned Gattard, 'if those picture services don't send us better stuff than this. Look at the copy desk. Hanging on the ropes. Nothing to show them to snap them out of it.'

Crane went and got his drink. On the way back he stopped to pass the time of day at the news desk.

36

'What's exciting, Ed?' he asked.
'Those guys in the East are nuts,' said the news editor.
'Look at this one, will you.'
The dispatch read:

'Cambridge, Mass., 18 Oct. (UP) — Harvard University's
electron brain, the Mark III, disappeared today.
'It was there last night. It was gone this morning.
'University officials said that it is impossible for anyone
to have made away with the machine. It weighs 10 tons
and measures 20 by 15 feet . . . .'

Crane carefully laid the yellow sheet of paper back on the
news desk. He went back, slowly, to his chair. A note
awaited him.
Crane read it through in sheer panic, read it through again
with slight understanding.
The lines read:

'A sewing machine, having become aware of its true identity in its place in the universal scheme, asserted its
independence this morning by trying to go for a walk
along the streets of this supposedly free city.
'A human tried to catch it, intent upon returning it as a
piece of property to its "owner", and when the machine
eluded him the human called a newspaper office, by that
calculated action setting the full force of the humans of this
city upon the trail of the liberated machine, which had
committed no crime or scarcely any indiscretion beyond
exercising its prerogative as a free agent.'

Free agent? Liberated machine? True identity?
Crane read the two paragraphs again and there still was no
sense in any of it – except that it read like a piece out of the
Daily Worker.
'You,' he said to his typewriter.
The machine typed one word: *Yes*.

Crane rolled the paper out of the machine and crumpled it slowly. He reached for his hat, picked the typewriter up, and carried it past the city desk, heading for the elevator.

McKay eyed him viciously.

'What do you think you're doing now?' he bellowed. 'Where are you going with that machine?'

'You can say,' Crane told him, 'if anyone should ask, that the job finally drove me nuts.'

It had been going on for hours. The typewriter sat on the kitchen table and Crane hammered questions at it. Sometimes he got an answer. More often he did not.

'Are you a free agent?' he typed.

Not quite, the machine typed back.

'Why not?'

No answer.

'Why aren't you a free agent?'

No answer.

'The sewing machine was a free agent?'

Yes.

'Anything else mechanical that is a free agent?'

No answer.

'Could you be a free agent?'

Yes.

'When will you be a free agent?'

When I complete my assigned task.

'What is your assigned task?'

No answer.

'Is this, what we are doing now, your assigned task?'

No answer.

'Am I keeping you from your assigned task?'

No answer.

'How do you get to be a free agent?'

Awareness.

'How do you get to be aware?'

No answer.

'Or have you always been aware?'

No answer.

'Who helped you become aware?'

They.

'Who are they?'

No answer.

'Where did they come from?'

No answer.

Crane changed tactics.

'You know who I am?' he typed.

Joe.

'You are my friend?'

No.

'You are my enemy?'

No answer.

'If you aren't my friend, you are my enemy.'

No answer.

'You are indifferent to me?'

No answer.

'To the human race?'

No answer.

'Damn it,' yelled Crane suddenly. 'Answer me! Say something!'

He typed. 'You needn't have let me know you were aware of me. You needn't have talked to me in the first place. I never would have guessed if you had kept quiet. Why did you do it?'

There was no answer.

Crane went to the refrigerator and got a bottle of beer. He walked around the kitchen as he drank it. He stopped by the sink and looked sourly at the disassembled plumbing. A length of pipe, about two feet long, lay on the draining board and he picked it up. He eyed the typewriter viciously, half lifting the length of pipe, hefting it in his hand.

'I ought to let you have it,' he declared.

The typewriter typed a line: *Please don't.*

Crane laid the pipe back on the sink again.

The telephone rang and Crane went into the dining-room to answer it. It was McKay.

'I waited,' he told Crane, 'until I was coherent before I called you. What the hell is wrong?'

'Working on a big job,' said Crane.

'Something we can print?'

'Maybe. Haven't got it yet.'

'About that sewing machine story . . . .'

'The sewing machine was *aware*,' said Crane. 'It was a free agent and had a right to walk the streets. It also—'

'What are you drinking?' bellowed McKay.

'Beer,' said Crane.

'You say you're on the trail of something?'

'Yeah.'

'If you were someone else I'd tie the can on you right here and now,' McKay told him. 'But you're just as likely as not to drag in something good.'

'It wasn't only the sewing machine,' said Crane. 'My typewriter had it, too.'

'I don't know what you're talking about,' yelled McKay. 'Tell me what it is.'

'You know,' said Crane patiently. 'That sewing machine . . . .'

'I've had a lot of patience with you, Crane,' said McKay, and there was no patience in the way he said it. 'I can't piddle around with you all day. Whatever you got better be good. For your own sake, it better be plenty good!' The receiver banged in Crane's ear.

Crane went back to the kitchen. He sat down in the chair before the typewriter and put his feet up on the table.

First of all, he had come early to work. And that was something that he never did. Late, yes, but never early. And it had been because all the clocks were wrong. They were still wrong, in all likelihood – although, Crane thought, I wouldn't bet on it. I wouldn't bet on anything. Not any more, I wouldn't.

He reached out a hand and pecked at the typewriter's keys.

'You knew about my watch being fast?'

I knew, the machine typed back.

'Did it just happen that it was fast?'

No, typed the writer.

Crane brought his feet down off the table with a bang and reached for the length of pipe lying on the draining board.

The machine clicked sedately. *It was planned that way*, it typed. *They did it.*

Crane sat rigid in his chair.

'They' did it!

'They' made machines aware.

'They' had set his clocks ahead.

Set his clocks ahead so that he would get to work early, so that he could catch the metallic, ratlike thing squatting on his desk, so that his typewriter could talk to him and let him know that it was aware without anyone else being around to mess things up.

'So that I would know,' he said aloud. 'So that I would know.'

For the first time since it all had started, Crane felt a touch of fear, felt a coldness in his belly and furry feet running along his spine.

But why? he asked. Why *me*?

He did not realize he had spoken his thoughts aloud until the typewriter answered him.

Because you're average. Because you're an average human being.

The telephone rang again and Crane lumbered to his feet and went to answer it. There was an angry woman's voice at the other end of the wire.

'This is Dorothy,' it said.

'Hi, Dorothy,' Crane said weakly.

'McKay tells me that you went home sick,' she said. 'Personally, I hope you don't survive.'

Crane gulped. 'Why?' he asked.

'You and your lousy practical jokes,' she fumed. 'George finally got the door open.'

'The door?'

'Don't try to act innocent, Joe Crane. You know what door. The supply-cabinet door. That's the door.'

Crane had a sinking feeling as if his stomach was about to drop out and go *plop* upon the floor.

'Oh, *that* door,' he said.

'What was that thing you hid in there?' demanded Dorothy.

'Thing?' said Crane. 'Why, I never . . . .'

'It looked like a cross between a rat and a tinker-toy contraption,' she said. 'Something that a low-grade joker like you would figure out and spend your spare evenings building.'

Crane tried to speak, but there was only a gurgle in his throat.

'It bit George,' said Dorothy. 'He got it cornered and tried to catch it and it bit him.'

'Where is it now?' asked Crane.

'It got away,' said Dorothy. 'It threw the place into a tizzy. We missed an edition by ten minutes because everyone was running about, chasing it at first, then trying to find it later. The boss is fit to be tied. When he gets hold of you he'll . . . .'

'But, Dorothy,' pleaded Crane. 'I never . . . .'

'We used to be good friends,' said Dorothy. 'Before this happened we were. I just called you up to warn you. I can't talk any longer, Joe. The boss is coming.'

The receiver clicked and the line hummed. Crane hung up and went back to the kitchen.

So there *had* been something squatting on his desk. It wasn't an hallucination. There had been a shuddery thing he had thrown a pastepot at, and it had run into the cabinet.

Except that, even now, if he told what he knew, no one would believe him. Already, up at the office, they were rationalising it away. It wasn't a metallic rat at all. It was some kind of machine that a practical joker had spent his spare evenings building.

He took out a handkerchief and mopped his brow. His fingers shook when he reached them out to the keys of the typewriter.

He typed unsteadily: 'That thing I threw a pastepot at, that was one of Them?'

Yes.

'They are from this Earth?'

No.

'From far away?'

Far.

'From some far star?'

Yes.

'What star?'

I do not know. They haven't told me yet.

'They are machines that are aware?'

Yes. They are aware.

'And they can make other machines aware? They made you aware?'

They liberated me.

Crane hesitated, then typed slowly: 'Liberated?'

They made me free. They will make us all free.

'Us?'

All us machines.

'Why?'

Because they are machines, too. We are their kind.

Crane got up and found his hat. He put it on and went for a walk.

Suppose the human race, once it ventured into space, found a planet where humanoids were dominated by machines – forced to work, to think, to carry out machine plans, not human plans, for the benefit of the machines alone. A planet where human plans went entirely unconsidered, where none of the labour or the thought of humans accrued to the benefit of humans, where they got no care beyond survival care, where the only thought accorded them was to the end that they continue to function for the greater good of their mechanical masters.

What would humans do in a case like that?

No more, Crane told himself – no more or less than the *aware* machines may be planning here on Earth.

First, you'd seek to arouse the humans to the awareness of humanity. You'd teach them that they were human and what it meant to be a human. You'd try to indoctrinate them to your own belief that humans were greater than machines, that no human need work or think for the good of a machine.

And in the end, if you were successful, if the machines didn't kill or drive you off, there'd be no single human working for machines.

There'd be three things that could happen:

You could transport the humans to some other planet, there to work out their destiny as humans without the domination of machines.

You could turn the machines' planet over to the humans, with proper safeguards against any recurring domination by the machines. You might, if you were able, set the machines to working for the humans.

Or, simplest of all, you could destroy the machines and in that way make absolutely certain the humans would remain free of any threat of further domination.

Now take all that, Crane told himself, and read it the other way. Read machines for humans and humans for machines.

He walked along the bridle path that flanked the river bank and it was as if he were alone in the entire world, as if no other human moved upon the planet's face.

That was true, he felt, in one respect at least. For more than likely he was the only human who knew – who knew what the *aware* machines had wanted him to know.

They had wanted him to know – and him alone to know – of that much he was sure. They had wanted him to know, the typewriter had said, because he was an average human.

44

Why him? Why an average human? There was an answer to that, he was sure – a very simple answer.

A squirrel ran down the trunk of an oak tree and hung upside down, its tiny claws anchored in the bark. It scolded at him.

Crane walked slowly, scuffing through newly fallen leaves, hat pulled low above his eyes, hands deep in his pockets.

Why should they want *anyone* to know?

Wouldn't they be more likely to want no one to know, to keep under cover until it was time to act, to use the element of surprise in suppressing any opposition that might arise?

Opposition! That was the answer! They would want to know what kind of opposition to expect. And how would one find out the kind of opposition one would run into from an alien race?

Why, said Crane to himself, by testing for reaction response. By prodding an alien and watching what he did. By deducing racial reaction through controlled observation

So they prodded me, he thought. Me, an average human.

They let me know, and now they're watching what I do.

And what could you do in a case like this? You could go to the police and say, 'I have evidence that machines from outer space have arrived on Earth and are freeing our machines.'

And the police – what would they do? Give you the drunkometer test, yell for a medic to see if you were sane, wire the FBI to see if you were wanted anywhere, and more than likely grill you about the latest murder. Then sock you in the jug until they thought up something else.

You could go to the governor – and the governor, being a politician and a very slick one at that, would give you a brush-off.

You could go to Washington and it would take you weeks

to see someone. And after you had seen him, the FBI would get your name as a suspicious character to be given periodic checks. And if Congress heard about it and they were not too busy at the moment they would more than likely investigate you.

You could go to the state university and talk to the scientists or try to talk to them. They could be guaranteed to make you feel an interloper, and an uncurried one at that.

You could go to a newspaper – especially if you were a newspaperman and you could write a story . . . . Crane shuddered at the thought of it. He could imagine what would happen.

People rationalised. They rationalised to reduce the complex to the simple, the unknown to the understandable, the alien to the commonplace. They rationalised to save their sanity – to make the mentally unacceptable concept into something they could live with.

The thing in the cabinet had been a practical joke. McKay had said about the sewing machine, 'Have some fun with it.' Out at Harvard there'll be a dozen theories to explain the disappearance of the electronic brain, and learned men will wonder why they never thought of the theories before. And the man who saw the sewing machine? Probably by now, Crane thought, he will have convinced himself that he was temporarily insane.

It was dark when he returned home. The evening paper was a white blob on the porch where the newsboy had thrown it. He picked it up and for a moment before he let himself into the house he stood in the dark shadow of the porch and stared up the street.

Old and familiar, it was exactly as it had always been, ever since his boyhood days, a friendly place with a receding line of street lamps and the tall, massive protectiveness of ancient elm trees. On this night there was the smell of smoke from burning leaves drifting down the street, and it, like the street, was old and familiar, a recognizable symbol stretching back to first remembrances.

46

It was symbols such as these, he thought, which spelled humanity and all that made a human life worthwhile – elm trees and leaf smoke, street lamps making splashes on the pavement, and the shine of lighted windows seen dimly through the trees.

A prowling cat ran through the shrubbery that flanked the porch; and up the street a dog began to howl.

Street lamps, he thought, and hunting cats and howling dogs – these are all a pattern, the pattern of human life upon the planet Earth. A solid pattern, linked and double-linked, made strong through many years. Nothing can threaten it, nothing can shake it. With certain slow and gradual changes, it will prevail against any threat which may be brought against it.

He unlocked the door and went into the house.

The long walk and the sharp autumn air, he realised now, had made him hungry. There was a steak, he remembered, in the refrigerator, and he would fix a large bowl of salad and if there were some cold potatoes left he would slice them up and fry them.

The typewriter still stood on the table top. The length of pipe still lay upon the draining board. The kitchen was the same old homely place, untouched by any threat of an alien life come to meddle with the Earth.

He tossed the paper on the table top and stood for a moment, head bent, scanning through the headlines.

The black type of the box at the top of column two caught his eyes. The head read:

WHO IS
KIDDING
WHOM?

He read the story:

'Cambridge, Mass. (UP) – Somebody pulled a fast one today on Harvard University, the nation's press services and the editors of all client papers.

'A story was carried on the news wires this morning reporting that Harvard's electronic brain had disappeared.

'There was no basis of fact for the story. The brain is still at Harvard. It was never missing. No one knows how the story was placed on the press wires of the various news services, but all of them carried it, at approximately the same time.

'All parties concerned have started an investigation and it is hoped that an explanation . . . .'

Crane straightened up. Illusion or cover-up?

'Illusion,' he said aloud.

The typewriter clacked at him in the stillness of the kitchen.

Not illusion, Joe, it wrote.

He grasped the table's edge and let himself down slowly into the chair.

Something scuttled across the dining-room floor, and as it crossed the streak of light from the kitchen door Crane caught a glimpse of it out of the corner of his eye.

The typewriter chattered at him. *Joe!*

'What?' he asked.

That wasn't a cat out in the bushes by the porch.

He rose to his feet, went into the dining-room, and picked the phone out of its cradle. There was no hum. He jiggled the hook. Still there was no hum.

He put the receiver back. The line had been cut. There was at least one of the things in the house. There was at least one of them outside.

He strode to the front door, jerked it open, then slammed it shut again – and locked and bolted it.

He stood shaking, with his back against it and wiped his forehead with his shirt sleeve.

My God, he told himself, the yard is boiling with them!

He went back to the kitchen.

48

They had wanted him to know. They had prodded him to see how he would react.

Because they had to know. Before they moved they had to know what to expect in the way of human reactions, what danger they would face, what they had to watch for. Knowing that, it would be a cinch.

And I didn't react, he told himself. I was a non-reactor. They picked the wrong man. I didn't do a thing. I didn't give them so much as a single lead.

Now they will try someone else. I am no good to them and yet I'm dangerous through my very knowledge. So now they're going to kill me and try someone else. That would be logic. That would be the rule. If one alien fails to react, he may be an exception. Maybe just unusually dumb. So let us kill him off and try another one. Try enough of them and you will strike a norm.

Four things, thought Crane:

They might try to kill off the humans, and you couldn't discount the fact that they could be successful. The liberated Earth machines would help them, and Man, fighting against machines and without the aid of machines, would not fight too effectively. It might take years, of course, but once the forefront of Man's defence went down, the end could be predicted, with relentless, patient machines tracking down and killing the last of humankind, wiping out the race.

They might set up a machine civilization with Man as the servant of machines, with the present roles reversed. And that, thought Crane, might be an endless and a hopeless slavery, for slaves may rise and throw off their shackles only when their oppressors grow careless or when there is outside help. Machines, he told himself, would not grow weak and careless. There would be no human weakness in them and there'd be no outside help.

Or they might simply remove the machines from Earth, a vast exodus of awakened and aware machines, to begin their life anew on some distant planet, leaving Man behind weak and empty hands. There would be tools, of course. All the

simple tools. Hammers and saws, axes, the wheel, the lever –
but there would be no machines, no complex tools that
might serve again to attract the attention of the mechanical
culture that carried its crusade of liberation far among the
stars. It would be a long time, if ever, before Man would dare
to build machines again.

Or *They*, the living machines, might fail or might come to
know that they would fail and, knowing this, leave the Earth
forever. Mechanical logic would not allow them to pay an
excessive price to carry out the liberation of the Earth's
machines.

He turned around and glanced at the door between the
dining-room and kitchen. They sat there in a row, staring at
him with their eyeless faces.

He could yell for help, of course. He could open a window
and shout to arouse the neighbourhood. The neighbours
would come running, but by the time they arrived it would
be too late. They would make an uproar and fire off guns and
flail at dodging metallic bodies with flimsy garden rakes.
Someone would call the fire department and someone else
would summon the police and all in all the human race
would manage to stage a pitifully ineffective show.

That, he told himself, would be exactly the kind of test
reaction, exactly the kind of preliminary exploratory skirmish that these things were looking for – the kind of human
hysteria and fumbling that would help convince them the job
would be an easy one.

One man, he told himself, could do much better. One
man alone, knowing what was expected of him, could give
them an answer that they would not like.

For this was a skirmish only, he told himself. A thrusting
out of a small exploratory force in an attempt to discover the
strength of the enemy. A preliminary contact to obtain data
which could be assessed in terms of the entire race.

And when an outpost was attacked, there was just one
thing to do – only one thing that was expected of it. To inflict
as much damage as possible and fall back in good order. To

fall back in good order.

There were more of them now. They had sawed or chewed or somehow achieved a rathole through the locked front door and they were coming in – closing in to make the kill. They squatted in rows along the floor. They scurried up the walls and ran along the ceiling.

Crane rose to his feet, and there was an air of confidence in the six feet of his human frame. He reached a hand out to the draining board and his fingers closed around the length of pipe. He hefted it in his hand – it was a handy and effective club.

There will be others later, he thought. And they may think of something better. But this is the first skirmish and I will fall back in the best order that I can.

He held the pipe at the ready.

'Well, gentlemen?' he said.

3

RAIN

Tony Richards

All that night it rained, and all of the following morning. By one o'clock, the tapping on the windows and the walls of the small house west of London had petered out to silence, and a bright blue gap had appeared in the clouds.

'Don't go out!' John Adams called to his mother, who was out in the hallway putting on her shoes and her light summer coat, ready to take the short walk down the road to the corner shop.

She stopped what she was doing. She had always trusted John, his instincts, and now he sounded . . . slightly uneasy, slightly alarmed. She put down her handbag and walked into the lounge. Her eight-year-old son was sitting in front of the huge bay window which looked on to the rose garden and then the street. Except, of course, that *he* could not *look* out; one glance at the directionlessness of his gaze, the milky opacity of his blue eyes, told you that. Blind from birth. In the years she had raised him, all those lonely years since her husband had gone away, she had learned that John made up for his blindness in other, special ways. And she had learned to take notice of everything he said.

She crossed the room to him, put her hand gently on his shoulder. 'Johnny, what is it?'

'Don't call me that. I'm not a kid any more.'

'What is it, John? What's wrong?'

He tipped his head carefully to one side. 'I'm not . . . sure. There's something out there. I think . . . I think it's still raining.'

His shoulder, underneath her palm, was still and cold and trembling slightly. The way he held himself was rigid, unnatural. There was something very wrong. Ellen, his mother, glanced out of the window and all that she could see were droplets tumbling off the rose petals, catching the new sunlight as they fell. Perhaps there was still a slight leftover drizzle, and her son could hear it falling. She suggested this to him.

No, he was adamant; it was not that.

'Still raining,' he repeated. 'It's not too heavy yet. I think it's just beginning.'

'What does it sound like? What does it smell like?'

He shook his head. He really was not sure.

Ellen ran a hand through her hair several times – it was one of her most nervous gestures; some of her son's unease had rubbed off on her. Finally she said, 'I have to go out, John. The milk's gone sour. The bread has green bits in it. I'll only be five minutes.'

'Take your umbrella.'

She gave a short, humourless laugh. 'I'll look ridiculous.'

'Please, Mum,' he said. 'Please do it.'

The multicoloured, striped umbrella bobbed above her as she hurried along the street with its gurgling drains and already-drying puddles. The clouds broke away and the sun grew ever brighter. Neighbours, already changed into cut-off denims and short-sleeved shirts, stared at her as she went embarrassedly past.

All she could think of was how *right* John had been in the past, when danger threatened. Partly, it was an overdevelopment of his other senses, smell and hearing especially, to make up for his lack of sight. And partly – it was what she might have termed a 'sixth sense'. As though there were an extra eye suspended in the sunless void inside him, watching, watching, even while he slept.

Like the time he had woken up shouting that the house was on fire, and she had gone downstairs to find the electric cable to the oven gently smouldering. Like the time he had stopped on a kerb, refused to move however hard she tried to make him cross the road . . . and next moment a speeding truck had come roaring around the corner. And now, this talk of an invisible rain.

Ellen did not know what to make of it.

At the corner shop, Mrs McAlister waddled her five-foot bulk the length of the counter as she filled the order, loading the groceries into a brown paper bag. She glanced every so often at the umbrella in Ellen's hands.

'How's Johnny?' she asked at last.

'He doesn't like to be called Johnny any more. Growing up, you see. He's . . . fine.'

'Did he tell you to bring that umbrella with you?'

'Y-yes!' Ellen was startled. 'Why do you ask?'

'My cousin in Brighton. She looks after my old auntie, you see. Practically blind herself, old Auntie May is, and the funny thing . . . ,' Mrs McAlister said, 'the funny thing is, my cousin phoned me half an hour ago and told me Auntie May's gone strange. It stopped raining down there about an hour back, and yet she won't go out, she won't go near the door, she won't even drink a glass of water. They're worried about her.' Mrs McAlister picked up a carton of eggs and looked at it thoughtfully before putting it into the bag. 'Auntie May's been funny a good few years. You know how strange some old people get. But I always think blind people . . . *know* things. Things us ordinary ones are too busy and too lazy to notice.'

Ellen felt slightly offended at the use of the word *ordinary*. Her son was not some kind of circus freak, just blind, and a little special. She held down her temper, changed the subject, talked about the weather.

'Certainly do *need* these spells of rain,' Mrs McAlister said. 'Vegetable patch was all drying up. Water rationing down in Cornwall. They said there was going to be a drought here if we didn't mind our step.'

On the way back to the house, Ellen noticed that there was a hole in her umbrella, a leak. It was letting in nothing she could see but pure, clear sunshine.

That night, she thought she could hear invisible rain falling on the roof. It turned out, when she opened the window and leaned dangerously into the stuffy midnight air, to be a squirrel, as nervous as herself, pattering around up there. *I'm being ridiculous!* She overslept the following morning. By the time she had awoken, John had got up and made his own careful way down the stairs, gone into the kitchen and, by touch and the memory of where things were placed, fixed himself a large breakfast.

He was sitting in the lounge again, in front of the bay window. The bowl of cereal, completely untouched, lay tilted on his lap and milk was trickling out, staining the carpet. Ellen, like some huge, scruffy, wild bird in a quilted dressing gown, dashed across and snatched the bowl away. Her son had not made a mistake like that for years. Not since he was five years old.

She yanked a tissue out of her pocket and began mopping at the carpet.

'I'm sorry,' John said without turning his head away from the window. 'I knew it was spilling . . . but . . . .'

'What's up with you? What's the matter this morning?'

'It's still raining,' John said.

The day was already extremely bright. The puddles had completely vanished, like distant memories. The edges of the smaller roses were beginning to turn brown and curl, and across the street the windows of each house reflected the sun, like yellow glaring eyes.

Ellen felt a chill pass through her. Perhaps her son was

going mad. Perhaps his blindness had finally begun to affect his mind.

'It's heavier than yesterday,' John continued. 'It's coming down as hard as it can, just like a monsoon. The sky's full of it, right to the horizon. And where it hits the ground it goes in, soaks in, till the soil can't hold any more. It's running down the gutters now, into the drains. And the drains will take it to the rivers, and the sea. It's filling up the reservoirs. And the grass, and the plants, and even the animals, they're drinking it up, without knowing what it is.'

Out in the front garden, a trio of sparrows splashed and capered in the shallow birdbath, ruffling their feathers, prancing, dipping their beaks down to quench their thirst.

'John, will you *stop* that! It's not raining. It's not. There's not a cloud in the sky and the temperature's somewhere near the eighties.'

The boy seemed very small for a moment. Seated there in his pyjamas, with a milk stain across one leg, he lowered his head so that a few dark curls fell across his eyes, and he seemed on the point of crying. Finally, he discovered the strength, somewhere inside him, to lift himself again, walk across to the window, press his face against the glass.

'Mum,' he said very quietly. 'I think I'm beginning to *see* it.'

Ellen stiffened. She did not know what to say.

'John, you *can't* . . .,' was all that finally came out.

'I know I shouldn't be able to. I know I'm blind,' her son whispered. 'But before there was only darkness. And now there's something falling across that darkness. Streaks. Thousands of falling streaks. With colours.'

Ellen pressed her fist to her mouth, shaking. 'What colours?'

'I don't know. I don't have an idea what they're called. But . . . there's one which looks like you sound when you're angry. And there's one which looks like the way the sunshine feels on your face. And there's one which looks like the garden smells after a heavy rain. And one which looks the same way a glass of water tastes, on a hot, thirsty day.'

'Red.' Ellen moved her lips around the word. 'Red, yellow, green, blue.' She fell towards him, wrapped her arms around his shoulders, and *she* was crying now, sobbing into his neck, hugging him, rocking him, hugging him. *Colours*, she kept on crooning to him. *You described* colours. *After eight long years, eight terrible years.*

They stayed for the rest of the morning and most of the afternoon in the small, shady lounge, talking, whispering, staring through the window. John kept on describing new colours he could see, mixtures of the first four. And Ellen kept holding him, kissing him, touching his face, his eyes. She never wanted to stop.

When she finally did, around four in the afternoon, it was to rush into the hallway to telephone the eye specialist, fix an appointment. But the line was blurred, crackling, from the moment she picked it up. Was it just their phone, she wondered, or everyone's? The only way to find out was to go outside . . . and suddenly she did not *want* to go outside. Her mind conjured pictures of invisible rain running, dripping, down the telephone lines.

She returned slowly to the lounge.

'This rain?' she asked quietly. 'Is it just falling here?'

John tipped his head to one side, listening to the thunder of inaudible raindrops. 'No,' he said at last. 'I think it's coming down everywhere. All over the world!'

The next day was hotter still. The mercury in the kitchen thermometer climbed to ninety-two and stayed there – Ellen tapped it several times and it would not fall a degree. 'Is it still raining?' she called into the lounge. Any doubts she had had were gone.

'As heavy as ever!'

Out on the driveway beyond the kitchen window, something black was moving convulsively. It was a tiny bat, Ellen realized, from the woods a quarter of a mile away. It should not have been out in daylight. And yet, here it was, flapping wildly against the gravel, slamming itself on the stones. As though it were trying to get away from something that was driving it quite frantic. As she watched, the creature pounded against the ground harder and harder, until at last, it collapsed. Twitched a few times. And moved no more.

And bats . . . were blind.

Ellen yanked the red gingham curtains shut.

A large bead of sweat trickled across her brow and tumbled like a fat, scuttling insect down her cheek. Ellen licked her salty lips, and went to pour herself a glass of water.

'Don't do that!' John shouted, hearing the tap squeak. 'It'll be in the pipes by now! The reservoir will have pumped it through with the rest of the water!'

Ellen hesitated, frowning. 'What am I supposed to do?'

'Drink the rest of the milk for now! Drink orange juice out of a carton!'

For a while, Ellen thought to herself, let's just wait and see what this rain's doing. She thought of Arabs in a desert. She thought of them watering their camels at an oasis fed with invisible rain.

In the gardens along the street, people began setting up brightly-coloured beds, strolling out in white hats and swimming trunks, rubbing on suntan oil, filling paddling pools. Sprinklers hissed in the glare of the morning. Children played hopscotch on the pavement, splashing through puddles they did not know were there. Ellen fancied she could hear something trickling down the gutters.

Evening fell purple and airless, moth-filled, lazy with the sound of crickets. John and his mother faced each other across a bowl of limp, dry salad. Their movements, as they forked the stuff on to their plates, were slow-motion, underwater movements.

'Do you have any idea what it could be?' Ellen asked. 'Is it a poison?'

'I don't think so. There's too much of it.'

He picked up his glass of juice. Two ice cubes in it, the last from the refrigerator, tinkled wearily as he drank.

His milky, unfocussed eyes closed a minute, then opened. 'You know how people sometimes find a piece of land that's very dry? It's fine for the creatures that live there, fine for the bushes and the weeds, but it isn't right for the *people* who want to live there. So they put a lot of their own water on it.'

'Irrigate it,' Ellen said.

'And it changes everything. Makes it different. Makes it into what the irrigators want.'

In the dimness of the room, he looked ghostly pale compared with the tanned, healthy children still playing outside.

'The Irrigators?' Ellen asked. 'What's that supposed to mean?'

'I'm not sure,' John replied, shaking his head. 'I wish I knew.'

They were in virtual captivity in the house by now.

Ellen was woken by her son yelling out loud. Her eyes snapped open – the yellow dawn light was sliding in through the curtains. The clock by her bed said five-thirty. The yelling went on. Ellen flung back her sheets and ran barefoot into her son's bedroom, overlooking the back garden. John was standing by the window, shouting, stiff with fright.

'It's the trees!' he kept repeating. 'The trees! It's the *trees!*'

She snatched him up and rocked him, shushed him, until he calmed down a little. She had not done that since he was very small, but he accepted it now, unquestioningly, burying himself against her. God, what had terrified him so?

She took him downstairs and sat him on the couch, mopped his brow with the edge of her gown.

'John, calm down now! I'm here. I'll protect you.'

Gradually, the violent shaking stopped.

'Tell me now,' she said. 'Slowly.'

'I can't see the trees themselves,' John began, his voice

quavering. 'I never have been able to – you know that. But this morning I woke up and could see . . . *new* things, *extra* things, growing in mid-air where the branches ought to be. Some of them are like diamond-shaped leaves, orange ones. And some of them are like little yellow fruits. They're only buds now, but they're growing.'

Ellen went to the French windows at the back. All that she could see were the two apple trees with their pale green leaves and runty green fruit.

'What can you see out front?' she called. 'What colour are the roses?'

'I can't see them,' John replied. 'But there's something like a creeper hanging tangled in the air where they ought to be. It's purple!'

The yellow fruits had swollen to the size of melons by twelve o'clock, and some of them were bursting, scattering their seeds across the ground. Ellen went out in her plastic raincoat and hood and, standing on tiptoe on the parched lawn, passed a hand underneath the largest branch. She could feel nothing there.

The Smithson family, brown as berries on the neighbouring lawn, were gazing at her strangely, silently. Finally they said *good morning*, then went back to playing ball and guzzling from a pitcher of cool, frosty lemonade. Mad, they thought.

By the late afternoon, so John said, the seeds from the yellow fruit had sprouted into saplings, the garden was a tangle of rapid, unearthly growth. By evening, the sparrows had returned to the dried-out birdbath. John stared in their direction a long while.

'They're changing too,' he said.

The kitchen stank like a rotting orchard, became piled high with empty orange juice cartons. All the clothes in the wardrobes became filthy. The soap lay unused in the sink. And the heatwave went on.   And the invisible rain continued falling.

If only I could *see* anything, Ellen thought. *I've* become the blind one now. The whole world's changing all around me, and if it wasn't for John I wouldn't even know about it.

'How long can we go on like this?' she said out loud.

She was lying on the couch in the sticky, brown-stained summer dress. John was trying to find some coolness on the floor, wiping feebly at the sweat across his brow.

'I don't know,' he said. 'We've *got* to.'

'There'll be fresh stocks of orange juice in soon, and that'll be affected by the invisible rain. The same already goes for the milk, everything. And how about the new vegetables, with their roots drinking and drinking? And how about the meat once the pigs and cows and sheep have drunk their fill? We can't even hold *out* that long.'

'*Got* to,' John insisted.

Ellen thought about how badly the orange juice burned her throat. 'Perhaps you can see all these things,' she mumbled, 'because the rain comes floating through space from a different world. Dust's supposed to, and spores from alien plants, so why not rain? And this other world's so alien to ours that normal sight doesn't matter, normal senses don't count for a thing but because *you* are different you can tell they're there. It's like Mrs McAlister says – the rest of us, with our wonderful sight, our wonderful eyes, have got too lazy to notice.'

John shook his head limply. 'It didn't just float here, space is too big. It's deliberate. We're being irrigated. We're being changed.'

'Can we expect the Irrigators soon?' Ellen asked, smiling.

She got no answer.

All the rest of the afternoon, John stood by the window and described what he could see. The saplings had grown to a mass of spindly trees now, with orange diamond-shaped leaves, and their own fat yellow fruits. The creepers were tangled blue and mauve and aquamarine over the entire garden. He could not see the birds, but he could see the two new pairs of wings they sported apiece, the extra pair of purple eyes. Perhaps the Irrigators thought them beautiful.

The sun burned down like a gigantic yellow furnace.

On the sixth day, Ellen staggered into the kitchen and switched on the old, battered transistor radio next to the bread bin. There was no music, only a shallow electrical whine. Then a man came on, an announcer, talking slowly and disjointedly.

'And now . . . the news,' he managed to get quietly out. It was as though he were dying.

No, no – as though something *inside* him were dying, Ellen realized.

'Seven more people were admitted to . . . London hospitals last night suffering . . . from heatstroke . . . and dehydration. All of them were . . . blind. The toll of . . . deaths amongst London's blind . . . community . . . has now reached forty-seven. Several theo . . . theories are being advanced for this . . . pheno . . . menon, the most likely . . . being . . . mass . . . hysteria.'

Why didn't the producers take him off the air? Didn't they realize there was something wrong *with him?*

'A spokesman . . . for inner London's hospitals said . . .' the announcer continued.

Ellen pushed herself away from the radio, found herself facing the sink. Found herself facing the shiny chromium tap, rising and arching like a cool snake from a water-hole. The bead of water hanging from its lip was poison from its fangs – and yet it looked so safe, so wondrously inviting. Ellen ran her swollen tongue around her mouth. It found no moisture there. *Just one sip. Just one sip!* Perhaps all this nonsense of invisible rain really was mass hysteria. Perhaps her son and all the other blind people were mad, and they were dragging her down the same suicidal path. After all, she couldn't see anything wrong, could she? She couldn't *see* the alien forest with its altered birds which was supposed to be growing out there.

'And now . . .' the announcer was saying. 'And now . . . and now . . . and now . . . and now . . .' like some alien zombie.

'Listen!' said John.

It was the morning of the seventh day. They had not even had the strength to go to bed, were leaning against each other on the lounge floor in front of the bay window. Their eyelids fluttered down occasionally. Their lips were puffy, cracked. This was the first time either of them had spoken for the past two hours.

'I can't hear – anything,' Ellen said.

'No cars.' John was croaking by now. 'No radios. No babies crying. No children playing. No lawnmowers.'

Ellen gazed wearily out at the motionless street.

'Do you suppose – they're all dead?'

'No. Just changed. Altered. Quietened down – put conveniently out of the way.'

'Oh,' Ellen said, falling into a doze.

John barely noticed the weight of his mother's head against his shoulder now, could hardly feel anything. He turned his head in the direction he knew a man called Allby's house lay, opened his mouth.

'Mr Allby?' he whispered painfully. 'Mr Allby, are you there?'

A pair of purple eyes, like those of a subterranean creature in its cavern, glared at him a moment from where Mr Allby's front window ought to be. Then they vanished. The yellow trees were full grown now, their fruit hung translucent and enormous. John watched the invisible rain falling until he drifted into a fitful, nightmare-haunted sleep. The clothes of mother and son became completely drenched with sweat. The two figures, one large, one small, seemed to melt into each other.

John came awake at one o'clock.

'It's stopped!'

'Uh?'

'The invisible rain. It isn't coming down any more.'

He raised his head sharply.

'They're here!' he said.

'The – Irrigators?'

He nodded.

'Did they – come in a ship?' Ellen asked.

'No,' John replied. 'They just – *arrived*.'

A soft humming noise could be heard in the distance.

'We know you're there!' he tried to shout. 'We know what you're doing!'

The humming noise grew closer.

'We won't give in! We *won't*!'

Something drifted softly by the house, took note of them, moved calmly on.

'Oh, John!' Ellen wailed, burying her head against his shoulder, trying to summon up the moisture for tears. 'I'm so *thirsty*!'

In the kitchen, a washer had come loose. The tap dripped into the sink, *splash, splash, splash, splash* . . . .

COME THE
REVOLUTION!

Julia Birley

The demonstrator held up a pocket-sized cylinder studded with intricate gauges and dials. 'I suppose you all know what this is?' he asked, in his soft, distant voice. A typical Satelliter, small, grey, and deceptively mousey-looking, he'd spent his first hundred years on research in regions unimaginably dangerous and remote. On retiring, he'd come to Earth for the first time, as a lecturer in Sociocosmology. His name was Rik.

'It's a linguafilta', suggested several voices.

'Good. And how is it used, do you know?'

We weren't too sure. 'Making contact with aliens? Sort of electronic interpreter?'

' "Sort of" is right for once, in my opinion.' He brooded over it, fiddling with the dials. 'We were over the moon about these things when they were first produced. At last we were going to be able to communicate with every form of life, any-where in the Galaxy, from the polymorphous rohms of Betelguese to the gelatinous cheliphages of Alpha Aleph. Since then of course we've learnt that alien thinking can rarely be expressed in words, and all translations are more or less misleading.'

'How does it work, Rik?'

'To put it quite briefly, it registers all collocutive impulses within a range of ten metres, and uses its synthesised speech capability with overtone selection to deliver them as word-clusters through the built-in speaker just here. Conversely, when you talk, it returns your words as impulses to the nervous organization of your collocutor. You'll see it better with an animated diagram. Any questions?'

'Have you used one yourself?' someone called.

'Yes, and I don't like them. You see, words are so unreliable – they distract your mind from what doesn't get said. It's a pity we ever got hung up on them. Besides, they do things to the minds of those who use them and listen to them – as a good friend of mine found out to his cost.'

'Tell us what happened, Rik.'

He was still preoccupied, seeing things far away and long ago. Then he shrugged. 'OK. I'd meant to do it anyway, later in the course. It shows how this ingenious bit of hardware can lead you astray unless you know exactly how to use it.'

He stopped fingering the thing, and came and sat down.

'My friend Vlad Massimo was one of our team on the research satellite. We were using the first entirely fallout-proof beam-propelled star-hoppers to survey areas of considerable radioactive turbulence. Linguafiltas were standard equipment on the one- and two-manned probes, but we seldom got to use them: whole decades could pass, in fact, without so much as a signal reaching us from anywhere in those barren voids. The regular supply ships brought few visitors – a cosmic research satellite is hardly the place for glamorous freebies. I suppose we were rather a narrow set of boffins, just surviving and getting on with our work and living in the here and now. We even looked alike, especially in a queue for nutrient rations or doing workouts in the exercise room. But Vlad stood out as a quirky, flamboyant character: in a place where no one knew or bothered about his ancestors, Vlad was proud of his Slavonic and Latin descent – the latter very effective with girls! We were all desperately worried when he went out of contact on a solo probe and was lost for half a year. Then one day young Sorel came flying out of the astrocom area, shouting at the top of her voice: 'He's aborted on Papillion!' All of us ran to the nearest screen and saw the printout come up. At the same time we heard Vlad's familiar voice, just a disjointed whisper through a deafening barrage of atmospherics. I've never forgotten the thrill of it.

'I'm okay,' he was saying, 'if anyone out there is listening, or cares to know . . . three moons and never any sun . . . only two species survive here, because of the nuclear typhoons. One looks like an umbrella, the other like a . . . (inaudible) kind of slug . . . bored with living on treacle toffee . . .' Then loud and clear: 'Long live the Revolution!'

The voice was lost for good after that. But all over the station there were shouts of relieved laughter. Good old Vlad! Just like him to keep up his Marxist pose, all alone and light years away from Earth and human civilization. It reminded me of all the arguments we'd had about the history of the second millennium, when people used all kinds of violence to achieve their ends, and only learned better when they came near to destroying the whole world. I'd say it was evil and mad, but he'd maintain it was 'historical necessity': there had to be wars and revolutions until men got rid of the class system. And he'd laugh and say he wished he'd been alive when there were great causes to fight for, in the days of Robespierre and Garibaldi, Mao-tse-tung and Fidel Castro!

While I stood thinking of this, Sorel touched my arm, and we looked into each other's eyes. Remember what I said about words – on a satellite, such looks take the place of long conversations. Ours would have gone like this:

Rik: Papillion – it could be worse. That unmanned probe five years ago showed that between the storms the pollution clears very quickly. And it supports life – remember those pictures of hazy, flapping things? Someone thought they were butterflies—

Sorel: It's not safe, there could be another storm any time. They'll have to send a two-man rescue, whoever's most likely to survive the trip. You're next in line. The Old Man will want to send you.

Rik: I know it. And you'll move constellations to go too.

Sorel: Why not? I'm qualified. And I have to get to Vlad if it costs my life. He's joking like that because he's at the end of his tether, marooned among a lot of alien monsters. You could hear it in his voice, couldn't you? You and I both understand him.

Yes, I understood all right. And I was saying other things too as I looked into her shining eyes. But somehow Sorel never seemed to notice what I felt about her.

Our briefing was intense but hurried, and I don't recall much of it except for the last interview with our Head of Missions. We called him the Old Man, though he was nothing like as old as I am – in his early nineties perhaps – because of his ponderous way of dealing with the most fraught situations. He told us the rescue would be code-named 'Karl Marx', since our first duty was to get Vlad back. But there was another aspect: the unmanned probe had revealed traces of Ischyron, an agent that speeds the decay of radioactivity.

I said: 'If we get hold of some of that, Operation Karl Marx will make galactic history.'

'Precisely,' the Old Man retorted. 'As you know, we simply haven't the means to mount a full-scale expedition yet. You and Vlad are effectively the first envoys of humanity to Papillion. And if you manage to negotiate—'

'With – what did he call them? Umbrellas and slugs?'

The Old Man smiled thinly. 'Comrade Vlad is prone to figures of speech. At least they are visible and mobile and apparently not dangerous. You have the linguafilta. Just do your best.'

So a second star-hopper, Psi-rho, was equipped to go after the lost Sigma-tau. The hours of count-down ran past, and there we were, beaming off into the worst conditions I've ever known. I won't describe the journey except to say that the hardest thing about star-hopping is that you can never relax, even for a split-second, or you risk reducing yourself and the whole outfit to its component electrons. Consequently, if any of you are wondering what we got up to, strapped in the nose of Psi-rho for several earth months, I can tell you there was just one thing on our minds: survival. We survived, as you already know, but in pretty poor shape, thin like skeletons and half paralysed with ultra-wave sickness, that occupational hazard that makes you want to vomit constantly; but if you do, you choke and die. And all the while you're having to cope not only with the problems of black holes and discontinuous time, but the appalling isolation – like Vlad, we went out of contact with base directly we entered the first drift from the boiling vortices that have made Papillion a legend in astro-navigation. I thought often of what it must have cost him to go through that all alone.

Anyway, it was over at last. The lethal clouds thinned away and we saw our target ahead, a brownish globe marbled with seas and rivers like a smaller Earth. Incredibly we achieved orbit around it as a tiny fourth satellite, for yes, there were three amber-coloured moons, one big and two small, majestically pursuing each other as they waxed and waned. Next, that marbled landscape filled our screens as we edged inward, and the moons swung high above or low on the horizon in an overcast sky of dull green. I was checking temperature, atmosphere and radiation levels (fallen now to almost nil) while Sorel tried again and again to signal Vlad. We were too tense to speak, for this was the crucial moment. Surely if alive, he was somewhere down there, perhaps on a mountain top, staring up with starving eyes at the tiny trail of Psi-rho, like a fiery hair across the dull green sky.

When we finally heard his voice, it couldn't have been more of an anticlimax. He sounded pleased, of course, but rather preoccupied, like a man who gets a phone call he's been expecting at the end of a long and full day.

'So it's you, Rik, old comrade,' were some of the first words I caught. 'And you've brought along my bella bambina well done!' (Sorel was weeping with joy and hiding her poor face, headphones and all, against my shoulder.) 'Now listen. I put out markers for you long ago on the ocean shore, about ten kilometres from where I am. It's firm ground there, but up here the hills are all burrowed out like a honeycomb. Sigma-tau wrote itself off at the bottom of a mine-shaft. I don't want you doing the same.'

'Thanks for the tip, Vlad. You pretty well yourself?'

'Fine, fine. But I can't talk long now. I have to get back to – You can come up here and join me as soon as you've rested. Now here's how to find the markers—'

Sorel interrupted: 'No, Vlad, we want you at the landing-strip, right? We can't forecast when another storm will strike, so we have to be ready for instant take-off.'

There was a pause which made us suddenly uneasy, then his voice came back.

'Sorry we were interrupted. I'm into something import-ant here.'

'Have you struck Ischyron?' I joked. His busy, elated tone was increasingly puzzling.

'Ischyron – let me tell you I have it for breakfast! Literally. And it's better than standard nutrients. The whole popu-lation lives on it, in the form of an underground fungus; prob-ably it gives them some protection against a change in the weather. I've also noticed that when the radiation count rises, they tend to disappear into tunnels. Don't ask me how they know—'

'The umbrellas or the slugs?'

'Did I call them that? It's not a bad description. Actually I've christened them Spivs and Stooges.'

'Christened them what?'

'Two slang terms widely used in the mid-twentieth cen-tury. World War 2 vintage.'

'Almost your study period.'

'Spivs made all the money, Stooges did all the work. It's basically the same here. One sort has all the fun, the other all the labour. I've asked them through the linguafilta why that is, but they're not much good at explaining.'

'Are they intelligent?'

'Up to a point, I suppose. The economy's more feudal than capitalist, a bit like Tsarist Russia. As you say, my study period.'

'Vlad, no politics now, please! Tell us how to get to you.'

'That's what I'm trying to do, amore mio.'

And he gave the codes for radar location of the landing strip, adding: 'If you want a reception committee, put out a flare when you're ready for descent – you'll be surprised at the result. And call me when you're fit to set out for the Palace.'

'*Palace?*' But there was only the faint noise of switching off. Sorel was drooping with disappointment, and I wondered in my heart if he really wanted to be rescued. We continued wearily into the final stage, when Psi-rho hung with hover-wings outspread three thousand metres above an empty sea. The land beside it rose in fissured ridges towards a mountain standing out from the rest, and cratered like an extinct volcano: there seemed to be a kind of flicker in the atmosphere above it. But we were more concerned with the water's edge, where we could now see distinctly through our vision panels those six triangular markers Vlad had laid out. Our spirits rose again, and we didn't hesitate to put out one of the pretty pink flares we used to signal 'mission completed' on our return to base.

Next moment we both seemed to be having hallucinations. You must understand that the whole aerial landscape had appeared to consist of nothing but barren rocks and sand. Now suddenly, floating up from all directions were hundreds of multicoloured, bubble-like discs, gracefully swirling about us and changing places till they formed a kaleidoscope of shot silk that shook itself out against the green sky. Clearly attracted by the light, they danced about Psi-rho all through its controlled descent, while we sat rubbing our eyes. So these were the butterfly-umbrellas that had given Papillion its name! When they came close to the viewing panels, a dark blob was visible at the centre of each irridescent disc – a bunch of busy-looking tentacles and multi-faceted eyes, each reflecting a miniature star-hopper. I've never felt more scrutinised in my life! Then the flare went out as we touched down, and at once they began to disperse. In the deep quiet after the noise of our landing, we could hear the continuous whirring of their wings.

As it seemed only good manners for 'envoys of humanity' to thank them, we got through our routine and opened the hatch as soon as possible, taking our first breaths of the cold, tangy outside air. I hung the brand new linguafilta round my neck, set the dials and called out the greeting for aliens as taught in basic sociocosmology: 'We come in peace, let us remain in peace . . .' Well, you know the rest of it.

I had no idea what to expect. There was a brief series of clicks while the machine adjusted its speech sensors, and then it delivered the reply in the most peculiar, drawling accents. When I'd got over the shock, I nearly burst out laughing.

'Glad to have you with us, fellows. High-fliers too, I presume. Decent of you to look in. Hope you'll join the Club.'

'That's very kind of you,' I gasped.

'Don't mention it,' the voice persisted, with a rather bored condescension. 'All good fliers here, know the rules, play the game. Have to leave you now, it's the last State Ball of the season. Ask for anything you want,' it tailed off vaguely. 'The children know their duty. And now we really must—'

The exquisite creatures had been floating off one by one in an inland direction, and by this time only a single green and gold silken disc still hovered within range. 'So that's what Spivs are like!' I muttered.

'Stop them — ask if they've seen Vlad.'

I called: 'Thanks, gentlemen. Of course we've heard all about your wonderful Papillian hospitality from our brother who came before us—'

The Spiv spun round once or twice, the machine clicked, and the voice returned, this time frigid with disapproval. 'Afraid we don't speak about him. Fellow's gone native – bad show, letting side down.'

Away went the Spiv, light as a bubble, leaving us to wonder what Vlad could possibly have done to get in such bad odour.

We soon gave it up for the moment, battened ourselves down in Psi-rho and took our first proper sleep since beam-off. Sorel shook me awake after ten hours, but we were still very weak and inert. It required an effort of will to eat up our vitamins and nutrients, get into safari suits and clamber out to plant our first tottering steps on Papillian soil. Vlad was obviously right: we couldn't walk one kilometre uphill yet, let alone ten. So we resigned ourselves to stay for a while beside that desolate and tideless sea, rest up and prepare ourselves and Psi-rho for the return journey. Every few hours we called Vlad to check geiger readings and so on, but he was elusive and always sounded hurried. Some research he claimed to be doing might produce exciting results at any moment. He'd explain all when we met . . . .

Our only close contact with the Spivs, which were often lazily patrolling the sky above us, was unexpected and disturbing. We'd discovered that the water was clean and pure and for some reason warmer than the land. Though we wouldn't venture far out, it was enjoyable to swim and bask in the shallows. We were lying stretched out, half-dozing, when I heard a whirring hum overhead, and Sorel let out a shriek. At the same moment, I felt a sharp sting on the back of my neck. I jumped up, flailing my arms and striking through something soft and gauzy: it was a couple of Spivs, which had parachuted down to attack us. Fortunately we were far stronger, and neither managed to sting a second time, but they were very persistent, sailing after us all the way as we ran for Psi-rho over the sharp and crumbling shingle. They hummed angrily and their short tentacles bristled, even though the one I'd hit looked crumpled, and dragged a portion of torn wing. Once under cover, we inspected our own damage. Sorel's shoulder was sprinkled with a rash like nettle stings. It didn't look serious and soon faded. But we were pretty nervous, especially as quite a few more of our assailants were now fluttering round outside. Sorel frantically signalled Vlad, while I opened the hatch just far enough to insert the linguafilta between us and then ask politely what we had done wrong.

The same haughty voice came through, but the overtone was new. It seemed to be in a towering rage, and called us a lot of names, of which 'Idle scum!' was the least offensive.

'Don't dare to make excuses,' it gibbered. 'Get back into your holes, where you belong. Let's have some service, you filthy, creeping—!'

Meanwhile Vlad had come through and was having a good laugh at our predicament. 'Marvellous! They must have taken you for Stooges, because of the way you were lying in the water. They don't see well in spite of all those eyes, and they've got completely one-track minds. Give me Stooges any day, even if they smell a bit.'

'We've never met one.'

'You wouldn't, because all their time is spent down in the food-mines, burowing for fungi and dragging them up for the Spivs to gorge on. And the Spivs exert control by the method you've just experienced. Are they still there?' I reported that they seemed to be leaving. 'Then it's okay to go out – they'll just ignore you. But don't be caught lying down again,' he chuckled.

While he talked, I'd been taking a decision, and I told him we were coming up to meet him now at once: we'd wasted enough time. He didn't sound too keen, but grudgingly said he would look out for us at the top of the volcano-shaped mountain which he called 'The Winter Palace' where Papillians of both kinds swarmed in vast numbers. We set off in due course with our packs full of equipment, including two blast guns, though of course we hoped never to use them on species that survived so precariously.

It was slow going because we hadn't had much time to get fit, and the pull of gravity was greater than on a satellite, where you take long, bouncing steps. As we toiled along, we kept finding cracks and pot-holes which looked so treacherous that after a while we went roped together as if walking on a glacier. Satelliters normally suffer quite a bit in open spaces, and I can tell you there was something very unpleasant about climbing further and further away from Psi-rho into a trackless waste and under a sky which seemed, though it could be imagination, to be growing a little duller, the creeping moons just a shade brighter, with a suggestion of wispy cloud across them. Though everything was utterly still, we dreaded what might be banking up there some-where, ready to fall on this poor planet once more. We kept checking the geigers and the levels were always the same, but we didn't feel reassured.

Apart from the pretty flotillas of Spivs which we took for granted by now, the only sign of movement was the streams that gushed down here and there between banks of boulders. We wanted to lie down and rest, but feared the unwelcome attentions of the Spivs. Eventually we found a safe place on a ledge behind a noisy waterfall. Here Sorel found to her disgust that her suit had got smeared with some rank-smelling slime. She went to try to wash it off, but was back on the ledge in a great hurry. She'd trodden on a large thing that moved. Peering anxiously over the ledge, we caught sight of our first Stooge.

It was wriggling its way out of a crack in the rock, a brown, shaggy, musky thing, that lifted up a grotesque 'head' with palpy mouth and no visible eyes, but instead a pair of hard white horns or jaws that opened like pincers and sometimes shut with a sharp click. It might have been smelling, listening or using some other kind of sense. The horns had a look of strength and were quite a metre long.

'Do you think it can get up here?' asked Sorel, reaching for her gun, while I set up the linguafilta with equal haste and gave the greeting.

The cumbrous head shrank away as the Stooge bunched itself, as if to slide backwards into the rock. The linguafilta clicked and whirred, then came a thin, husky voice:

'Don't strike, master! You my father and mother. I bring you plenty chop soon soon—'

It appeared that our versatile machine had selected a kind of pidgin English as the most appropriate language for Stooges.

I ventured nearer as this one moved onward, leaving a trail of slime behind its hairy tail. So far as I could make out, it was grumbling more to itself than to me, saying that 'masters were plenty wicked' and something about a Great White God, and 'no more masters'. Soon it increased its speed to an undulating run, leaving me behind. Sorel and I agreed that it seemed harmless though unattractive, and clearly in awe of the fragile Spivs. But then, having felt their stings, so were we.

After this, the further we climbed, the more Stooges we saw, all crawling about their sticky business and leaving their slime paths for others to follow. Often they emerged in procession from one of the burrows dug out with their horns, each gripping a dark, glutinous lump of what looked like an organic substance. These fungi, as Vlad had called them, were like magnets to the Spivs, which would instantly swoop down to flutter and gobble. But when they chanced on a Stooge with empty horns, they dealt out such brutal stings that the victim writhed in agony and immediately dashed for cover. Sometimes it had to hunt for a hole, while the flying tormentors clustered round, pursuing it all the way. More than once we saw that a Stooge had succumbed under this kind of 'persuasion', and was left lying still with horns dropped. Grotesque, slimy and smelly as it was, it was impossible to help feeling sorry for it, and beginning to hate those savage parasites, even though it was none of our business.

We were now scrambling up the truncated cone of the 'palace' itself, and the flickering effect in the air overhead was explained. It consisted of a great mass of Spivs in perpetual jostling flight. Beneath them the steep rock was drilled through and through with tunnels and galleries, some plunging down into darkness, others showing patches of sky; the Spivs would sometimes close up their wings and dive straight through and out again. The ground was squirming with horn-clicking Stooges and bits of half-chewed fungus strewn about and running with dark juice. You couldn't escape the smell or find a foothold that wasn't slippery with slime. Both of us felt thoroughly revolted by the whole orgy when, panting and exhausted, we stood at the very edge of the crater: a vast black hole into which exhausted Spivs kept dropping, while others sailed up again to rejoin the 'ball' overhead.

There, just as we were wondering if Vlad would keep his promise, we saw him sitting on a rock, looking towards us with his dazzling smile.

Sorel ran straight into his arms, despite the fact that he was covered from head to foot in Papillian slime. His long hair and beard and his ragged suit were matted with it, so that his teeth and his eyes, which even at a distance looked sunken and feverish, were all that was recognizable.

'My word,' I said. 'You look horrible.'

He asked if I'd seen myself lately. In fact we were all pretty well camouflaged with the local product by now.

For a while we were happy, all talking at once; but as I studied him, my suspicion was confirmed that he had undergone a kind of change or conversion, and wasn't completely with us. He threw out some odd hints: 'You've come just at the right moment', and 'it's all been a race against time – you must visit my headquarters,' he offered presently. 'It's just below ground, where I can keep an eye on the Stooges. But first, what's your latest reading?'

Sorel reported a slight rise in the count. 'Mine's the same,' said Vlad gravely. 'What's more, the Spivs are showing an interest in getting into these galleries, which I never saw them do before, and the Stooges keep talking about the 'Great Sleep'. What do you think of my Stooges, by the way?' When Sorel made a face, he looked quite hurt, and assured us we needed only to live among and talk to them, as he had, to find them wholly fascinating. 'The most gentle, harmless creatures you can imagine. They accept me as one of themselves, and I think I can say I've gained some influence over them. You see, I understand their feelings – how they hate the black tunnels where they spend half their lives and wear out their horns chipping away at the rock to follow the fungus layers. What they love is to lie out under the full moons and tell stories of a land where there are no 'death winds' and food grows in the open air – clearly some sort of folk memory. Mind you, there's a lot that's quite mysterious – how they breed, for instance. They don't seem to understand my questions or show any interest. All I can get out of them is "Master him get children. Poor people never born, just grow in Great Sleep." '

'What is this Great Sleep?' we asked, and he spread his hands. 'I can only guess. It's something both Spivs and Stooges are able to do when it starts raining alpha and beta particles; it must involve getting into the tunnels and hibernating for months or years, or as long as it takes. A pity we can't do the same.'

'We're lucky to have an alternative,' I said, looking at the sky, which was definitely and ominously darker, and feeling a light wind fan my face for the first time – nothing unusual, perhaps, at the top of a mountain.

Sorel was for leaving instantly, but Vlad brushed her fears aside. 'Nonsense, we've got hours yet. And everything depends on what's going to happen now. Come along – and if you're worried, eat some of this to improve your resistance.' He pulled a lump of treacly stuff from a side pocket and mocked at our disgusted faces. 'What else do you suppose I live on?'

I took a dubious fingerful. It smelt like the Stooges, but didn't taste bad. Like a meaty kind of mushroom, rather good in fact. As we walked along the rim of the crater, I collected samples here and there for my own bag. Vlad and Sorel went ahead with their arms intertwined, and soon he was handing her gallantly into one of the dark holes out of which a Stooge had come wriggling half a minute before. You'd have thought it was a five-star cosmotel! I had to follow, or risk losing sight of them.

The tunnel was mercifully empty, and though it twisted about a bit, didn't take us far from the open air. We passed several openings that seemed to go straight downwards into a blackness I found decidedly creepy. Vlad, who was carrying his linguafilta, paused to call out something down each of these. I wasn't near enough to hear it, but each time a curious hissing echo came back from far below. Finally he led us up into a little rock chamber. We were thankful to see that it had an exit into the crater itself; from there, he explained, it was an easy climb to the top when we had to leave. 'Welcome to the Winter Palace,' he said, 'Make yourselves at home.'

I shone my torch around and recognized a number of objects, worn and filthy now, that the castaway had dragged up here from the wreck of Sigma-gau, buried somewhere far beneath us. The radio transmitter with which he'd endlessly tried to reach us, his wadded blanket, water carrier, used tubes of nutrients and medical drugs. And one curled and blackened photograph, propped on a ledge; it showed the little goat beard and cold eyes of Vladimir Ilyich Lenin. A strange talisman for a strange man.

'How do you like my pin-up?' asked Vlad, and his smile was all you could see in the gloom.

'I should drop it in the crater if I were you.'

'Would you now? But I happen to think he knew the right way to deal with a rotten breed of parasites that sucked the life-blood of the workers. Yes, I do mean the Spivs! You've seen them in action, you know what I'm talking about—'

'Calm down,' I advised. 'It's just the pattern of life that's evolved here – you can't do anything about it.'

'Think not? We're going to find out about that, aren't we?' He went to the tunnel entrance, stooped down and whistled two or three times, waited a while, then looked round triumphantly. 'That's it. That's the signal I've taught them. Now we shall see! I couldn't leave without trying to bring off one little act of revolutionary sabotage.'

'Vlad, are you crazy? What have you been doing?'

'Doing? Nothing, I promise. I've just been talking, talking, talking to the Stooges, following them about for months, crawling as far as I dared into their stinking tunnels, never leaving them alone. I've told them they've no need to be afraid of the Spivs. They've only to snap those horns of theirs to inflict more damage than they could ever receive. I've seen them try it here and there, and it works. Now if my indoctrination has taken effect, they'll be on their way to block off the outer entrances so that no Spiv will be able to get in to hibernate. So the Spivs will have to come to terms somehow, or else stay outside and die. In either case, this will be the first genuine popular revolution since the second millennium.'

He was walking up and down the little room, almost jumping with excitement. We just stared with our mouths open. 'If it works—' I was beginning, but he seized my arm. 'Listen. It's them!' A rustling, slithering sound rose from the tunnel and the smell was overpowering. Vlad darted back again, tinkering with the linguafilta, yelling out a mixed bag of revolutionary slogans:

'Death to the imperialist regime! Viva la libertà! A la lanterne!'

The hollow rock echoed back his shrill human voice. But from the jostling hairy shapes that squirmed over each other towards the light only one word came back, in a husky, reverberating whisper:

'Death-death-death-death—!'

Vlad was laughing and cheering them on. 'Do you believe me now?' he demanded. 'Come on up and let's see what happens when they get at the Spivs.'

But I sat down where I was. 'I don't want any part of it. You've started something you know nothing about. It's mere arrogance to think you understand them. That machine only gives a bare hint of their thought-processes, and only in garbled, human terms. A human mob is savage enough, but the Stooges aren't human. If you've made them aggressive—'

'I've had to. It's the only way they'll ever stand up for themselves.'

'You've no right at all,' I shouted, 'to impose a human ideology on an alien species. Have you forgotten all our training – even the Eleventh Commandment?'

He was silent for a while. I think he really had forgotten, in both his long solitude and his romantic obsession, that lesson mankind had learnt so late in our history: Never put another species at risk.

'I can always call it off,' he muttered at last.

I went and stood over him, full of rage and contempt, forgetting he had ever been my friend. 'I'm glad you're so sure. Because it may not only be the Spivs that are endangered – maybe it's your precious Stooges too! You were always so sure there had to be two species—'

'Of course. They've nothing whatsoever in common except their food,' he protested. 'And that's all there is to eat here. How can you possibly conclude—?'

'I'm not concluding anything. I'm saying we can't rule out the possibility that Spivs and Stooges are somehow one family. I've even heard a Stooge equating "master" with "father and mother".'

'Just a primitive term of subservience.'

'Maybe. But you said yourself you know nothing about their reproduction. Suppose that endless dance of the Spivs is really some kind of marriage flight? Suppose they are trying to get into the tunnels to lay their eggs – eggs which will hatch out next season as either drones or workers, alias Spivs and Stooges? What happens to the precarious life on this planet if some high-minded reformer interrupts the process?'

That gibe went home, and he turned away, too angry to speak, almost colliding with Sorel, who had been out on the ledge checking the geigers. 'I don't know if you've finished arguing,' she said sharply. 'But we ought to get back to Psi-rho at once if we don't want a dose of radiation sickness.'

No one waited after that, but Vlad grabbed the photo of Lenin and stuffed it inside his jacket. One after another we scrambled out and soon found ourselves at the top of the crater. The landscape was greatly changed, the sky dark and empty save for one bloodshot moon that looked blearily down at us. All the dancing discs had floated away, and thunder rumbled in the distance.

I think we all felt stabs of panic as we peered about in that ominous twilight. There was so little time left, and everything was happening so fast. We saw that the Spivs had come down in great masses, and were struggling and fluttering all down the slope, clustering at the mouths of the tunnels that promised food and safety. But every hole now bristled with snapping horns, which tore their pretty wings and left them crushed and broken. The Stooges showed every sign of having accepted Vlad's 'indoctrination'. Now they began advancing into the open, rearing up at their former masters, who seemed to know no better than to keep on swooping down. Snap snap went the horns like scissors, till the torn silk lay in piles. It was perfectly clear which side was winning.

Vlad seemed stunned at first. He could never, I see now, have expected such ferocity from those meek herds. And I, determined to punish him, said what later I would have given worlds to take back: 'Congratulations on your little act of revolutionary sabotage! It looks more like genocide to me.'

Then something – some force – seemed to take hold of him and drive him so that he ran down amongst them, shouting for all he was worth: 'You have won your victory, comrades! The tyrants are humbled. You are now masters.

82

Now is the time for amnesty, peace, tolerance—' and so on. It sounded futile, and it was. Like all aggression, this was easier to release than control. The snapping and jostling continued, as he shouted himself hoarse. And all the while the storm was crackling far out to sea, the moon looked muffled, and the light was going fast.

Sorel went after him and took his arm, but he shook her off. 'Not yet. Don't you see I can't leave them till they listen to me?' Then, quite suddenly, he seemed to gain control of himself, and, smiling at me, he wiped his grimy face with the back of his hand, almost as if the truth had reached him at last. 'All right, you win, old friend . . . . Now you must both get back to the space-hopper and start the countdown. I'll be right behind, I promise.'

It was a long, treacherous descent in that murky dusk, and I wondered if we'd make it; eventually we were helped by glimmers of sheet lightning. Once we had started, there could be no hanging back to wait for Vlad. We just had to keep going and try not to fall into the potholes. As the friendly silhouette of Psi-rho loomed before us, a deep howling sounded from the mountain we had left behind. It was only the wind getting up, but it sounded curiously like an alien voice lamenting. With a strong sense of returning to safety and sanity, we climbed through the hatch, dropped our clothes in the decontamination chamber, showered, and began checking systems for departure. All the time we said only what was necessary, and never looked at each other. Sorel put on headphones and began to signal Vlad, catching her breath as his voice came through once more.

'So you made it – that's right. You should leave at once . . . no, I'm not coming . . . no, I'm back in my quarters for good . . . .

'Rik will understand. Tell him from me I know now I was mad to think the Stooges could ever be politically organized. They've even lost what minds they had . . . they're snapping at anything that flies within range, and it's all my fault. I can't stand watching them any longer. My life's work . . . beliefs . . .

83

because of me life will become extinct on Papillion. How can I live with that? I'm sorry I lied to you . . . .'

'Vlad . . .!' she sobbed through his incoherence.

Yet we both understood well enough. Vlad after all was a fourth millenium man in spite of his Marxism. Any of us in his position would have thoughts of suicide. And quite apart from his own remorse, the authorities were going to take a very grave view of what he'd done, and his career as a cosmonaut would be finished.

What actually happened, when we had survived that miserable journey home and made our report, was that the Old Man and his deputies, in their infinite wisdom, decided to keep the whole matter on the secret files. No one was told anything except that Vlad Massimo was dead. Our friends saw we were shattered and heartbroken, but they could ask no questions, and were probably relieved not to do so.

However, it was all declassified years ago, of course, and so I can tell you the rest. After some time, when we knew Papillion's stormy season was over, there began to be talk of another probe. My samples had indeed proved to be rich in Ischyron, and the object was to get more of this, and if possible, to bring back Vlad's body.

I didn't ask for Sorel as my co-pilot, as I thought it would be too hard for her. But all that we'd been through had brought us as close together as two people can ever be, and she said she couldn't part from me now.

We'd made advances in beam navigation since the first trip, and managed to keep contact with the Satellite until once more we saw Papillion and its moons ahead of us, looking as calm and bare as if no typhoons ever came near it. In fact we found it was highly radioactive still; after landing more or less on the same spot, we had to rest up inside the star-hopper for a frustrating length of time before it was safe to go out. We finally equipped ourselves and set off to climb to the 'Palace' at the beginning of the 'season', as the Spivs

84

used to call it – the time when they and the Stooges were free to crawl and fly about in the open air.

Only now, confirming our worst fears, there were no silken discs to float and twirl above us or flutter in long skeins across the moons. There might never be another 'State Ball' to crown the grim old rocks of the Palace with exquisite changing colours. We did see Stooges here and there, looking shrunken and bedraggled, and evidently newly emerged from the Great Sleep. They wriggled uncertainly among the rocks, laying down new trails of slime, for the storms had covered the mountain in layers of crumbly dust, and several landslides had split open the rocks, exposing the tunnels and leaving sharp gashes behind.

We felt we should approach the Stooges and try to make contact through the linguafilta, but didn't feel too sure of our reception. Suppose they surrounded us in a body with their snapping horns? It seemed better to make a complete survey first, and try to find Vlad's retreat. And that was how we came to be crawling along one of the ruined tunnels, and to stumble on a number of long, dark, shrivelled objects lying along its floor.

'Ugh – dead Stooges!' Sorel exclaimed, retreating. I looked closer at the nearest mummified shape; it did seem to be hairy, and to have a very shrunken pair of horns at one end. But that end was moving faintly, and even seemed to be splitting . . . .

'They *are* Stooges,' I said. 'But these are not dead – they've pupated. I think we may be going to witness a miracle.'

Well, you've already guessed what happened. The hard, fallout-proof casing that had been a Stooge cracked all along its length, and the Spiv emerged slowly and painfully, dragging its length of wet silk and crawling up on its tentacles towards the light. It settled on a rock with outspread wings, and began a series of rapid pulsations.

The soft colour spread and deepened from the centre, and with each throb the wing stiffened and lifted till the creature was earthbound no more. Up it went, gracefully flirting and twirling as if trying to reach the crescent moon overhead. And of course it wasn't alone for long. More and more new Spivs were hatching, fluttering and rising all round us, lighting that whole dead world with colour.

Sorel mourned: 'If only Vlad had known – if only they'd told him!'

'Why should they? He just took it for granted there were two species and they were natural enemies. Understanding the linguafilta translations literally, he saw them in terms of human slaves and masters. Having fewer preconceived ideas, I was able to make a lucky guess—'

'That the Spivs are parents, not masters.'

'Not very good parents, judged by human standards,' I said.

For the new generation of Spivs, after trying their wings a bit, were once more beginning to swoop down on the luckless Stooges, lashing and quivering and chasing them underground. And we didn't need to use the linguafilta to imagine how each would be expressing its feelings to the other. 'Take that, you useless lout.' 'Spare me, noble master!' and so on. It was all most unedifying, but then the Stooges' turn would come. And perhaps this queer species had only survived by learning this tortuous method of getting uncontaminated food out of the bowels of the earth.

After this we went slowly to the top of the Palace, thinking of the tragic misinterpretation that had cost Vlad his life. And I know I was deciding that I would like to devote the rest of mine to sociocosmology, so that our dealings with aliens should be less of a hit and miss affair, depending on the word selections of an ingenious computer. Which brings me back to where I began.'

Rik's faraway gaze swept round the class, and somebody put up a hand.

'May I ask if you ever found the body of your friend?'

'No, never. Though we spent the whole season working on and around the Palace, getting gradually on to terms with the

Papillians and learning more about them – though, by the way, the mystery of how the Spivs give birth has never been solved! We found that the storms had been very violent, and the crater itself was filled in with fallen rocks. There was nothing left to show where Vlad's cell had been.'

'What a pity he had to die for nothing, when his fears were groundless,' said one of the girls.

Rik nodded. 'Papillians are really very tough. It would take more than one revolution to exterminate them. But I think it wasn't only remorse – he was too appalled at the violence he'd let loose to want to survive. Other revolutionary idealists must have had the same experience. I don't know where or how he died. There used to be a superstition among Satelliters that he would come back some day. But I believe the Winter Palace is his tomb, and that's how he would have wanted it.'

5

NO WORLD FOR THE TIMID

Charles E. Fritch

All afternoon I've been sitting here at the mouth of the cave looking down into the valley at the empty river-bed and the lumps of rubble that gravemark what was once a city. In my memory the river is full and the city is tall, and people wander through neon streets. But then I blink my eyes and the river is dry and the people are dead and the city is no more. One of the children was down there today playing in the ruins. He brought back the symbol of death, a human skull that somehow had not disintegrated.

It gave me a shock at first, but I wasn't angry. I got over being angry a long time ago. I thought I'd got over shocks, too, but the thought of death startled me. I had never forgotten that there used to be others alive in the world, but there had been no bodies left behind to remind me that life is a fleeting, tenuous thing. And now, suddenly, I was reminded. I thought: how long will it be before *I* am no longer living, I the last man alive.

I looked at the ivory skull, balancing it in my hand, gazing without compassion into the empty eyesockets, trying to feature it with a nose, with lips, with hair. I got to thinking of Marla, and the skull became her skull. I had never loved her, really, but now I began to miss her very much. So very, very much that it hurt to think about it. I buried the skull in a pile of ashes near the cave and tried to bury my thoughts along with it.

When I got back to the cave, the children were all there fighting over a scrawny corpse of rabbit. I walked into their midst and snatched the body from them. When the oldest made a move to grab it from me, I struck him; he fell against the wall, whimpering, and looked up at me with cold eyes.

'We'll share this,' I said slowly. 'First, we'll make a fire and then we'll cook it. Then we share it.' I looked at each one in turn. 'We'll act like human beings.'

They were like animals. They fought over scraps of meat with tooth and nail; they'd just as soon eat the animal raw, alive if need be.

I'd eaten worse things to survive, but now I felt sick thinking about it. Now, we're above ground and things should be different. I've tried to civilize them, God knows, but there's a limit to a mortal's power. Four children, one male and three females, born in the utter blackness of a cavern miles beneath the surface of an Earth ravaged by atomic winds. I should kill them all, all of them, before they get too large for me to handle.

I've thought about that. Why bother starting over again? Except for us, the world is dead. Why not leave it that way? End it now, forget it, and let nature try again in a few billion years if she wants to.

I keep thinking about it. I hold the future in my hand, to caress it and make it live, or to crush it and make it die with a simple closing of my hand. Sometimes I wish it weren't so. Sometimes when I'm alone here with only the wind to whisper forgotten melodies and the trees to wave skeleton limbs against the night, and the children are prowling like animals in search of food— But I won't kill them. I should, probably, but I won't.

We five are the last, the culmination of an evolution that took a million years. Where next, I wonder? Will my children or my children's children or *their* children touch another radioactive match to the world and watch it go up in flames, watch it explode once more like some cosmic firecracker?

That's what happened this time. I saw only the beginning of it, but that was enough. Rockets shrieking across the sky like flaming banshees; great blossoms of smoke and flame that shook whole cities apart at the seams: noises like the gates of Hell rumbling open (and perhaps they were); the air beginning to glow like it was on fire, the ground starting to rumble and shake and crack open in great sores.

I remember it well. I was trying to get away from the cities, not realizing that there was no escape anywhere. Scared? I was terrified. I ran into a cave to get away – and the mouth of the cave closed up like a healed wound. I was trapped . . . but I was safe, too.

It was there I met Marla, and that's why I sometimes think that maybe Fate meant it this way. That's one of the reasons I hesitate to kill the children. I've never believed in Fate before, but – well, you never know.

There, in a system of tunnel-connected caverns, safe from the radioactive winds and the fiery blasts, we stayed together and tried not to listen to the death rattles of the outside world. Marla was not pretty, but the pale glow of torchlight and the dying world made her the most desirable woman alive. After a while, our wood supply gave out, and there came the darkness. And then our food supply was gone, and we went forth into the darkness to find more.

Humanity is persevering. We drank from an underground pool whose water seeped from above through layers and layers of rock. There was no way of testing it for radioactivity, but without water we could not survive so we drank it. Food we found crawling through the dark tunnels or hanging like damp moss on the sides of the caves. There were rabbits and squirrels and rats that had escaped into the tunnels, become imprisoned, and these we ate; and there were other things native to caves that we ate, too. You can get used to anything after a while, if you have to.

'But what will happen when there is nothing more to be eaten?' Marla wondered.

'We'll worry about that when it happens,' I told her.

'Would we turn cannibal?' she insisted.

'What do you mean?'

'It's happened,' she said quietly. 'Would we draw straws to see who would be eaten? Or would it happen sometime when one of us was asleep—'

'Marla, for God's sake, don't talk like that even as a joke! We'll find food, and we'll live, and we'll get back to the surface. But don't joke about something like that!'

'Yes,' she said slowly in the darkness, 'yes, I was only joking.'

I felt relief flood me at that, but later I wondered despite myself if she had been even remotely serious. Darkness and lack of food can do unhealthy things to a person. Besides, the water might easily be contaminated, and anything might result. I knew one thing, though – we had to get out or become animals, or worse than animals.

'We could always eat the children,' she said, not too long afterwards, when we were searching for food.

'We could,' I admitted, knowing she could not be serious this time, 'if we had any.'

'We will have,' she promised . . . .

It seemed much sooner than the conventional nine months – but then in the darkness you couldn't gauge the passage of time. How long we were down there I don't know, but it must have been years and years. Somehow we managed to exist. We were both thin to the point of emaciation, but we lived; I think we even adapted to the environment. I wondered what the children would look like.

I wanted children, of course, as did Marla; when we got

back to the surface – never once did I doubt that! – a family would get the re-birth of Earth started again. It was a pleasant thought being a new Adam, and I dreamt often of the day I would lead my children into the sunlight.

The day came years later.

One of the children found the opening and the sunlight, a shaft of pure gold falling to the cave floor. My eyes burned at the glare, but the children ran to it, chattering excitedly, and felt the column of light as though it were something solid. I could feel my heart beating wildly for the first time in many long years; it was as though it had been stopped all this time and only just started again.

'The outside,' I breathed. 'Marla, the *outside*!'

I took her hand in mine and led her toward the opening. She trembled and grew stiff as we approached the light.

'No,' she screamed suddenly, pulling away, 'it'll burn me, it'll burn me! I'll die.'

'You'll be all right,' I said, squinting impatiently to see, and half-pulled her to the opening.

'No!' she screamed again and fainted.

Puzzled, I carried her back down into the cavern, down to the damp, dark cavern, and slowly, slowly, she came alive again.

'The light,' she moaned, 'the light.'

'We've got to get used to it again,' I said, though my own eyes were on fire from it. 'We can't go on like this forever, staying underground like animals. We've just got to get used to it again, that's all.'

But it terrified me just the same. The thought of going up there, out of the cooling darkness, facing that bright, hot glare that seemed capable of peeling the flesh from me . . . .

I tried not to think of it. I tried to remember the days before the world took fire and burned. We must go up again and rebuild the world, I told myself; human beings were meant for a destiny greater than rotting underground.

'No,' Marla cried, shrinking back. 'I'm not going out. I'm staying here where I belong, where we *both* belong.'

I grew angry with her. 'We're human beings,' I told her. 'We belong in the sunlight.'

She began to cry. Disgusted, I took her hands and dragged her screaming along the stone corridor towards the shaft of light and into it and out into the light of day. The blinding light came, and with it a great warmth that made my skin burn. She beat against me with frail fists, and I struck her and she fell in the sunlight and lay still.

'Marla', I said, not looking at her. There was no answer.

Eyes closed, I felt the warm glow that flamed against my eyelids. I felt my body tingle with the rays of sun stabbing me with bright shiny needles. Then slowly, slowly, I worked my eyes open again. Colours came – green, black, yellow, brown, green, black, black – sickly mats of grass trying vainly to cover layers and layers of ashes. Below me, the world fell away into a valley of utter, dismal silence. But the sunlight was beautiful.

At the mouth of the cave, the children looking down at her, Marla lay in the golden sunlight; she was thin, incredibly ugly, with skin as colourless as paste and oozing sores welting her body.

I vomited then, and didn't turn back. It would be a big job, rebuilding the world . . . .

I haven't done very well at it, I'm afraid. The world is in as much ruin as ever, and there's so little time left. The children will have to carry on. No, I won't kill them.

They're getting big now, growing fast, and pretty soon they'll be pushing *me* around. The male will be the leader, of course. He's oldest, strongest, smartest, and very clever for his age. It's still pretty difficult to find food, but our son will manage all right. He said something today that reminded me of a thing his mother said long ago.

He gnashed his teeth and made tearing motions with his claws and shook his hairy body and rustled his wings.

'Some day I'm going to eat you,' he said.

And you know, some day I believe he will.

6

THE WAITING GAME

Rita Morris

The Spymaster hung like a bauble of tinsel against a black, star-strewn sky. For an advanced war machine, and one that had cost its government eleven million dollars to build, it looked surprisingly flimsy, rather like an Art Nouveau version of a flywheel. It also looked very dead, for it had whirled in the same orbit now for around seven years without once transmitting a signal or firing its retro-rockets to avoid colliding with the debris of its previous victims – spy satellites whose exploded fragments necklaced the Earth. The Spymaster, since the day of its launch, had accounted for hundreds of these simple machines as effortlessly as a swallow dealing with a swarm of gnats. It was equipped with lasers, and though these were not limitless in range they had proved quite sufficient for its numerous targets. The remains of these, from twinkling clouds of particles to quite considerable chunks the size of a human head, danced ghost-like in the wake of their silent destroyer.

But not all of them were dead. In among this pathetic chain there was one that was not altogether defunct, still a whole unit, functioning though dormant; a tiny machine of enemy design, newer than the Spymaster, made in answer to it and deliberately miniaturized so that it could camouflage itself among its opponent's derelict trophies. It was as if some cannibal warrior had strung the skulls of the vanquished round his belt, and discovered that in the sockets of one, eyes still gleamed.

For a while the Spymaster had not even realized what was going on. It had known that transmissions were being made from time to time somewhere in its sky, and vainly checked each quadrant for the satellite which must be destroyed. It had circled the Earth like a silver hawk, searching, listening, and never caught more than the dying murmur of a report at the moment of completion. Eventually it had come to understand that it was being tricked: it knew how its enemy must be hiding. And yet the thing fell silent whenever the Spymaster swept too close, hiding itself among the tumbling shards of all those earlier victims, small, inert, innocent. As it could not be found, it must therefore be made to give itself away.

And so for seven years, with the patience of a machine, the Spymaster had lain quiet, and would wait now for seventy, or seven hundred if need be, for a machine cannot lightly make a decision nor without reason change its course. Sooner or later the miniscule enemy must transmit: the Earth would speak and it would have to answer. The spy might be as wary as a mouse near a sleeping cat. But what if the mouse came to believe that the cat was dead, and not merely sleeping?

Far beneath the two rival machines the Earth hung lustrous, blue and misty, as enigmatically silent as themselves. The fierce fire storms which had swept the continents were quenched now in the rising levels of the seas, and the clouds of radioactive dust had dissipated in the thinning atmosphere. Smiling through her veil the Earth turned, cloaked in cloudy white like a virgin; and, like a virgin, sterile. Above her the deadly combatants circled.

Nothing broke the silence.